I liked to watch them. It was interesting, the way they went about their day to day lives. Some actually caring what they did, others...not so much but there was one that interested me above all others.

She was the life and soul of the party whenever she walked into a room, her smile could cheer up the saddest of men and she had a laugh that sounded like she loved life and life loved her back but this just wasn't true and I was the only one who could see her when the mask slipped and she was alone; when she would kick her bedroom door closed and slump down on her bed and just cry. How she would pull at her shoulder length hair and mutter to herself about feeling worthless and stupid. It was heartbreaking to watch.

As an Angel you get to see a lot of things that other humans don't and I liked to watch this human in particular. Of course I had to be careful, if the other Angels saw that I was favouring one human above all others then I would be reprimanded and maybe even banned from keeping watch over her, so I used to watch her when I knew everyone else was busy watching over their allocated humans. You see, if you make your way up in Heaven and you're ambitious, you can become a Guardian Angel, assigned to a human to help him or her through their life but the human is one that the Arch Angels pick; not you, hence my hesitation about becoming a Guardian Angel.

If I couldn't protect and guide her then I didn't want to protect or guide anyone.

One day I did something that would get me into trouble if I was caught;

I went down to Earth...

She took the cut through to the park like she always did on her way home from work but this time she stopped, sat down on the grass and cried. Her head on her crossed arms as she hugged her knees to her chest. The sobs wracked her body and I felt physical pain blossom in my heart at seeing her like this. I couldn't help it. My heart broke for her.

I went down to the park and settled in a patch of trees where I concentrated on shedding my shimmering white aura and robe then winced as my wings retracted and I took on the guise of a normal human being; hoodie, jeans and trainers; I could have been a college student for all   she knew.

I came out of the clearing and stood to the side, wondering how I would approach her.

As I stood watching her, I suddenly wondered what my reason for seeing her would be. It didn't matter, I had to know why she was so sad. This girl who always looked so happy, was crying and I wanted to know why. Who or what had hurt her so bad that she was crying in a park on her way home.

I walked up to her and stopped to stand by her side as she quickly wiped her eyes and sniffed.

"Are you ok?" I asked, looking down at her.

She sniffed again, forced a fake smile onto her face and looked up at me, nodding her head but her bright blue eyes were shining with unshed tears.

"Yeah, I'm fine." Her voice thick with emotion.

I gave her a sympathetic look which earned me a frown.

"You don't look fine." I said softly.

The frown turned into a glare, her eyes turning to ice.

"What's it to you?"

Ooh, anger. I had seen her display this emotion before but never had I seen it first hand, it was a little unnerving to say the least.

I softened my tone.

"Nothing, I guess. Look, I was just passing through but I don't really know my way around. Could you tell me where the bus station is?"

I have come to Earth and now I have lied. How many more rules must I break?

She nodded and got to her feet, wiping the grass stains from her work trousers.

"I'm going there myself. You can tag along if you want." She muttered, sniffing again.

I nodded and gave her a bright smile.

"Sure. Thank you."

We walked side by side to the bus station which was a little walk but I wondered why she was getting on a bus when her home was just around the corner from the park. The silence was becoming a little awkward and I glanced up at her, seeing as she was at least a few inches taller than me.

"So erm, what's your name?"

She didn't even look at me as she answered;

"Natasha."

I smiled.

"Natasha...that's a nice name."

She shrugged.

"It's alright. What's yours?"

"Morgan."

She stopped and looked at me but there was no smile, no sign that knowing my name did anything for her.

"It's pretty."

I blushed at the compliment.

"Thank you."

That awkward silence descended again.

"So Natasha, what do you do?"

"Me? I work part time at a newsagent."

"Oh that sounds like fun!"

I actually had no idea what she was talking about. I knew what a newsagent was but working in one? Not a clue.

She arched an eyebrow at me.

"It's really not. All it is, is stacking shelves, watching kid-thieves and sorting out newspapers. Ohh though from time to time, I get to empty the bucket that's been collecting the water from a hole in roof for what feels like a decade." She said rolling her eyes.

I brightened, completely missing the sarcasm.

"So you have some responsibility. Must mean they trust you."

She stopped walking again and looked at me.

"Sarcasm isn't your strong point is it?"

I blushed again, feeling stupid that I'd missed her tone.

"N-no."

She sighed then carried on walking.

I wanted to know more about her and found myself firing questions at her like an overly enthustiastic but very polite detective. She didn't seem to mind answering my questions though.

I asked about her family, where she lived and her hopes and if she had any dreams for the future.

She told me that she lived at home with her family -mum, dad, a sister and two brothers- but she hoped to move out into the city soon, somewhere more modern with diamante covered furnishings and a glass balcony.

I'd heard her tell this fantasy to many people over the years and it never changed from one year to the next.

She wanted to get out of working at the newsagent and become a therapist as she liked listening to people and thought she could help them. I couldn't help but admire this in her.

"So what about you, Morgan? What do you do?"

Oh crap. I hadn't thought that she would be asking me questions too.

"Oh well, I'm a er- a-a waitress."

Waitress. Good going. As if you even know what they do.

I could practicaly hear my brain rolling it's eyes.

"A waitress...where?"

"City of London. It's a small little cafe, you wouldn't know it."
She looked at me and a smirk touched her lips like she was being issued a challenge.
"Oh really? What's it called?"
Bugger.
"The-the Perly Gates."
The smirk turned into an amused grin.
"The Perly Gates? As in Heaven? Those perly gates?"
I nodded, swallowing and choosing to stick with my ridiculous story.
"The owner thinks he's god."
She laughed at that and I inwardly winced. If anyone really was watching me, they would have me on that god comment.
Least I'd made her laugh though, that had to be worth it.

When we reached bus station, she stopped and looekd at me again.
"This is it. What bus you getting on?"
I glanced at the buses and picked one at random.
"So where are you going?" I asked her.
She sighed.
"Boyfriend's place."
"Boyfriend?" I asked.
I had never seen a boyfriend in all the time I'd been watching her. When did that happen? I know I couldn't watch her all the time but surely I would have seen something.
She rolled her eyes and smiled sadly.
"Yeah boyfriend. He's shit, unreliable and a pig but it's somewhere to go."
I frowned.
Ok so she wanted an escape but going to see a boyfriend that didn't treat her right?
Plus I didn't want this to be the last time I saw her- with her knowing I mean- don't get me wrong, I wasn't a pervert; I never watched her in the shower or in bed, I normally went away when that happened

but I just didn't want to not ever talk to her again. There had to be something I could do.

Without thinking I grabbed her hands in my own and looked into her eyes.

"Don't go."

"What? Why?" She asked, looing understandably panicked.

"Because you are worth so much more than that. You have to know that...don't you?"

She shrugged. Non-commital.

"Well you are. You don't need to do this just..." I searched for words, for an excuse, anything and I grabbed the first one that came to mind.

"Come for a drink with me and we'll talk...about anything, everything, whatever you want."

She smiled and looked down at my hands still holding her's.

"We don't know each other. Why do you care?"

"I just do."

She stared into my eyes for a very long time, almost as is she was trying to read me. Finally, she looked down then nodded as a small smile crept across her face.

"Alright. Let's talk."

Things progressed quickly after that. I snuck down to Earth every chance I could to see her and be with her. She didn't know what I was and I wasn't sure that I could tell her without getting into big trouble.

I always had an excuse when the timing to see her got difficult; 'I was working late', 'someone called in sick and I had to cover their shift', 'They offered me overtime and I couldn't say no', she understood thankfully but I wondered how long I could keep this up before she stared asking questions.

One evening, when I managed to get away, we were walking through the park I had met her in and she stopped and looked at the setting sun, smiling to herself.

"Do you know it's been six months today since we met in this very park?"

I nodded, smiling up at her.

"I know."

"Who knew you could make friends during a chance meeting in a park?"

Friends? That's what we were?

I frowned, looking down at the grass, trying to sort out my feelings; I thought I liked her as more than that but maybe she didn't...

"Morgan?"

I looked up.

"Yeah?"

"You've gone quiet. What's wrong?"

I licked my lips.

"Is that all you see us as?"

"What?"

"Friends."

She shrugged.

"Well it's been six months and we haven't kissed so..."

"You want me to kiss you?"

She blinked and looked away, like she was asking herself that question.

"I dunno...maybe?"

Maybe?

Well this was romantic.

I began to feel very unsure of her, like maybe I'd read the signs wrong and being friends was as far as this was going to go and I should just accept that. So I held my hands up and took a step back from her.

"Look, if you don't wan-"

That was when she grabbed me by the front of my jacket and pulled me flush against her, pressing her lips to mine as she squeezed her eyes shut.

I returned the hard and unexpected kiss and let her break it.

She kind of pushed me away and then stood there, breathing hard and looking at me like she couldn't believe what she'd done; her eyes impossibly wide.

"I think we've successfully fucked up our friendship."

She seemed unsure but me? I was over the moon.

I moved towards her, taking her hands in my own.

"I think we've made it better." I said a little shyly.

She bit back a grin and licked her lips.

"Ok, so maybe I like you a little more than a friend."

I couldn't help smiling brightly at her and she rolled her eyes with that same small smile on playing on her lips.

"We are so not the same when it comes to things like this."

I shrugged. That didn't matter to me; I loved Natasha for who she was, the good and the bad and I decided that it was time to tell her as much.

I swallowed my nerves and looked up into her eyes.

"Natasha?"

"Yeah?"

I looked down for a second and then back up at her. I knew I loved her. My heart had been screaming it for ages, even before we'd met, I'd just never listened as I didn't think us becoming anything was possible but now that I thought there might be a chance, even if it was just a tiny one, I had make my feelings known.

"I'm in love with you."

She blinked, the smile dropped and her lips parted in shock.

Maybe it was too soon, maybe I shouldn't have said anything, maybe this was a big mistake and I should've just kept my mouth shut.

She wasn't saying...why wasn't she saying anything?

Oh no. No, no, no, I messed up. I need to fix it.

"Sorry. That was too soon- I shouldn't have said anything-"

She held up a hand and stepped back from me. She was frowning now. Not good.

"You're in love with me?"

I swallowed and nodded my head slowly.

"How long?"

"How long what?"

"When did you know? Was it just after we kissed? Before that? What?" She snapped.

"B-before."

"How long before?"

That was another question altogether.

If I told her the truth then that would mean confessing what I was, that'd been watching her without her knowledge for ages and she wouldn't appreciate that or maybe she wouldn't even believe me. Then what?

I looked down, knowing that when I looked back up, her eyes would have narrowed and turned to ice.

"Morgan, how long?" She repeated, tone firm.

I sighed.

She was going to find out some day. It might as well be today.

I looked up at her, staring straight into those ice blue eyes.

"A long time."

"You think six months is a long time?"

I shook my head.

"Before that."

"You didn't know me before that."

"Yes...yes I did."

Her frown deepened but at least now she just looked more confused than angry.

"I'm not following."

"I'll show you but not here. Can we go someplace more private?"

She nodded, looking a little perplexed. She took my wrist and pulled me towards the same patch of trees that I had used to hide in while I changed into a more human form.

Ironic didn't begin to cover it.

Once she felt we were definitely hidden from view, she stopped and turned to face me, arms folded.

"Ok. So what do you have to show me?"

I let out a breath, feeling more nervous than I'd ever been.

Then I shrugged out of my jacket, letting it fall to the ground and then closed my eyes, focusing on the skin on my back; it had to shift in order for the wings to break through.

I moved my shoulders a little as I felt them wanting to push forward. This was...hard. I hadn't done this many times; maybe like, twice? I concentrated hard, seeing my wings come through in my minds eye, then when I was sure they would come through on their own, I focused on my aura. How it shimmered around me, lighting me up like a warm light that sparkled. Then the white robe. My human clothes dissovled, leaving me naked for a just a second until the white robe materialsed on me and my wings burst from my back, almost touching the ground.

I let out another breath as the transformation became complete and then raised my head, opening my eyes.

Natasha was staring at me with tear filled eyes.

I frowned.

"Why do you look upset?"

She swallowed and shook her head.

"I never thought...how can you be-"

"An Angel?"

She nodded mutely.

I was human once. I don't remember much of my life but when I died, I became an angel, like everyone does who goes to Heaven. Some of us choose to watch over the humans on earth...I was one of them." I said with a slight shrug.

"But-but how can you be down here? Angels aren't supposed to come down here and reveal themselves to humans."

I cocked my head to one side, a confused but suprised smile on my face.

"You know a lot about Angels."

"I read." She replied, a little sharpness in her tone.

"Why are you here? Why are we...seeing each other?" She asked haltingly.

"I was watching you. I have been watching you for a long time, Natasha. I liked you, I do like you. I broke the rules and came down here because I wanted to talk to you. I thought just talking to you that day would be enough but after spending some time with you, I realised I didn't want to leave. So I've been sneaking down here, every chance I can get just to spend more time with you and now...now I'm here, on earth as an Angel and I'm in love with a human. I'm in love with you."

She stared at me, her eyes unblinking, lips slightly parted and her posture unreadable.

She also wasn't speaking.

"Nat? Please say something." I begged quietly.

She licked her lips and frowned a little.

"So what does this mean for us? If you're an Angel you can't stay on earth with me."

"Do you want me to stay with you?" I asked and I couldn't keep the hope from my voice or the earnest expression I knew I wore.

She shrugged and I chose to see it that she didn't know what to say because she wasn't sure what I wanted to hear.

"Do *you* want to stay with me?"

I nodded.

"I do...I really do. I want a life with you, Nat. I want to remember what it was like to be human. I want to share that with you."

She looked down at where my jacket had fallen and nodded her head.

"Ok...so what will you do?"

I straightened. I'd been thinking about this for some time; I knew it was a big ask but if they could see how much I loved Natasha, maybe they'd let me stay here with her.

"I'll go back to Heaven, talk to Darius, the head Arch Angel and tell him I've fallen in love and I want to stay with you on earth and live out my life as a human."

Her frown deepened.

"Will they accept that?"

"I don't know but I have to ask."

I moved forward and cupped her cheek, her skin felt so warm against my palm.

"You're all I want, Nat. I just have to make them see that."

I pressed a kiss to her lips and then pulled back.

She looked at me then, really looked at me.

She gestured to my wings.

"Can I?" She asked, reaching out.

I nodded and she moved forward as I slowly turned. She ran her fingers lightly over my wings and I could feel her touch on the soft, white feathers. She then ran her hand over my bare shoulder and down my arm as she came to stand in front of me once again.

When she looked into my eyes, I blushed.

"What?"

"I always thought you were beautiful but this...you're something else."

I tilted my head down and she hooked two fingers under my chin to raise my gaze to her's.

"Come to bed with me."

I stared at her, eyes wide.

"You want...?"

She nodded.

"Don't you?" She asked.

I found myself nodding back.

She then snaked her hand down my neck and then my arm until she was holding my hand.

"Let's find a hotel."

I frowned.

"A hotel?"

"Yeah. Well we can't go back to my place."

"Why?"

"Because my family are there and they-they don't know about you."

I blinked.

"They don't?"

"No."

She then laughed and shook her head.

"Can you imagine if they knew I was going out with a girl?! And then I'd admit that that girl was an Angel?! I'd never hear the end of it!"

I frowned a little.

"But if Darius lets me go, I'll be human and then you won't have to tell them the Angel part."

She looked me up and down quickly then smirked.

"Yeah but you'll still be a girl."

"And that's a problem?"

"In my house it is."

I didn't understand and I wanted to ask more questions but Natasha was insistent, making it obvious she just wanted us to find a hotel room.

"I need to change back first."

She shrugged and then walked out of the clearing while I began to transform back into the disguise of a human, all the while thinking that her family didn't have a clue that their daughter was out right now with another woman.

TWO

I had never seen Natasha so eager about anything; but this, this was different. We found a hotel, a cheap but nice enough room and as soon as I crossed the threshold and the door was shut, she was on me.

She spun me around and grabbed me, pulling me into a fierce kiss that left me panting for breath as she tore at my clothes.

I put my hands on her shoulders and pushed her back a little.

"Nat. Nat slow down, we have all night."

She ignored me, unzipping my hoodie and pushing it off my shoulders. She then kissed me hard again and went for the zipper on my jeans.

Once again, I pushed her back.

"Why are you rushing this?"

"I want you, Morgan." She said with a shrug but her eyes were on my tank top that had ridden up to expose my stomach.

"I want you too but we can take it slow, okay? This doesn't have to be rushed. It should be special...because you're special."

Her gaze darted upwards and for a split second, I saw something soften in Natasha before a muscle in her jaw twitched and she looked strong again.

"I'm special?" She said with a smirk.

"Yeah. You are."

She grabbed hold of my hips and pulled me against her, making me blush.

"Then kiss me."

I did but I went softly this time, closing my eyes, savouring this moment, savouring her.

For a while, Natasha followed my lead, seeming to enjoy the gentleness of the kiss; the way we explored each other's mouth and lightly nipped at each other's lips, grinning as we did it.

When we broke apart, I took a step back and pulled my top over my head, tossing it on the floor.

She stared at me as I then unzipped my legs and shimmied out of them; letting them fall to the floor and kicking them away.

I swallowed my nerves as she stared at me, drinking me in.

"You're beautiful." She breathed.

I blushed.

"So are you."

She gave me this haughty look, that smirk coming back onto her face.

"Really? You think so?"

I nodded.

"I really do."

She bent her head to kiss me again and this time, she guided my hands, helping her undress. I let her show me how to undress her. Once we were both in our underwear, we stood back and looked at each other.

I stuided her expression; she wanted this there was no doubt about it but she had this softness in her eyes that I rarely saw.

"I love you, Natasha." I said quietly.

That softness seemed to vanish after a second and suddenly, she was pushing me back onto the bed, kissing me roughly as I laid beneath her.

I tried to get her to slow down but she didn't seem to like that idea and as soon as she had lifted her lower half off of me enough, she pushed her hand down my underwear and touched me. I knew I was wet and she grinned when she felt it too.

Finally, she pulled back, smirking down at me.

"You say you want me to slow down but your body is telling me something else."

I blushed and squirmed with embarrassment.

She used the hand that was down my pants to hold me where I was.

"No, don't shy away from me now." She said teasingly.

"It just...I'm embarrassed."

She bent her head and swiped her tongue up the side of my neck.

"Don't be embarrassed. It just shows how much you want me. I think it's hot."

"You do?"

She nodded.

"Yeah, now open up for me baby, let me take care of you."

I forced myself to relax as she slid a finger into me. I gasped, the sheets buching in my fists as she started a punishing rhythm. I was glad I was so wet as I'm sure it would've hurt otherwise.

It didn't take long before I found myself close to coming.

"You're close aren't you?" She teased, adding another finger.

I nodded, biting my lip.

"You don't have to be quiet here, Morgan. People come to hotels to hook up all the time."

I swallowed, trusting that what she was saying was right.

I found myself moaning when she re-doubled her efforts, sending me over the edge as I came hard. Stars exploded behind my eyelids and my back arched completely off the bed as my inner muscles clamped down on her fingers; almost like I was scared she would slip away from me if I let those fingers go.

When I opened my eyes again, I found her grinning down at me.

"Feel good?"

"That was...amazing." I panted.

She chuckled and then flipped us so that I straddled her. I looked down at her, unsure of what to do as she rested one arm under her head, looking up at me.

"What do you want me to do?" I asked, wanting so desparately to please her.

"Kiss me."

So I lent forward, capturing her lips and kissing her passionately. When she needed to catch her breath, she gently pushed me back.

I licked my lips as I stared at her. She had this knowing grin on her face.

"Now it's time for you to return the favour."

I moved my hand towards her underwear when I felt her put gentle pressure on the top of my head.

"Not like I did."

I frowned in confusion.

"Then like what?"

She grinned darkly.

"Use your mouth."

Oh...Ohh.

I grinned back up at her before she pushed down on my head untill I was right where she needed me to be.

The next morning, I awoke to the sun streaming in through the window of the hotel room. It was peaceful and I rolled over to find Natasha already awake and looking up at me; bright blue eyes wide and sparkling.

"Good morning."

"Morning." She practically purred and stretched, letting out a small moan which had me thinking back to last night and how she'd moaned then.

I sat up and rested back against the headboard, the pristine white sheet now covering my body.

"So, last night was..."

Natasha smiled and rolled onto her stomach, giving my arm a playful bite as she looked up at me.

"Yeah, who knew it could be that good with a woman."

I chuckled and ran a hand through my hair.

"I think it's more to do with the fact of who you're with and how deep the love is."

She prodded my side and grinned.

"Aww, look who's getting all romantic."

I blushed and nudged her under the covers with my knee.

"Shut up."

"You love me." She teased as she sat up, getting in my face.

I surged forward and kissed her into silence.

I pulled back and gave her a little grin of my own.

"Yeah, I do."

Her cheeks flushed pink and chuckled.

"You're adorable when you're embarassed."

She poked me in the side again, making me flinch and then rolled onto her back beside me.

"I wish we could stay here."

I sighed as I linked our hands.

"Me too."

She let out a louder sigh.

"But I have to go back to my parents."

"And I have to talk to Darius about giving up my claim as an Angel."

She nodded as she looked down at our entertwined fingers.

"Morgan?"

"Hm?"

"We're doing the right thing, aren't we?"

I frowned a little in confusion.

"What do you mean?"

"Well, me, coming out to my parents and you, giving up your right to live in Heaven. In case you haven't noticed, Earth? Not all that great."

"You're here, aren't you?"

She blushed again.

"Come on, be serious."

"I am."

I turned to face her and brushed some hair back from her eyes.

"If you didn't exist on Earth, I wouldn't want to give up being an Angel. You are my soul reason for doing this, Nat. I love you."

She smiled and looked down like she was shy.

"And how about you? How do you feel about coming out to your parents?"

She shrugged.

"Had to happen sooner or later, right? At least this way, moving out will be easier. It's not like they'll beg me to stay once I admit I've fallen for a girl."

She didn't sound happy that she knew this about her parents and I could understand that.

Natasha, above all else; just wanted to feel loved.

I hoped my love for her could be enough to make her feel whole where she hadn't been before.

Darius was standing in front of me, his muscular arms folded and a stern expression on his face.

"We know what you've been doing, Morgan."

I swallowed, licking my lips nervously and wringing my hands.

"That's actually what I came to talk to you about."

He stood there, his dark eyebrows knitted together.

"I'm waiting."

I took a deep breath.

"I know what I did was wrong and there is no excuse for what I did but all I have is the truth."

"And that is?" Darius pushed, one eyebrow arching.

"I fell in love, Darius."

I shrugged when he didn't comment.

"I didn't mean to but I was just watching her one day and...I fell for her. I went down to Earth- as you know- and we've been spending time together. She loves me and I-"

"Are you sure?" Darius cut in.

I frowned.

"Am I sure what?"

"That she loves you."

"Of course she does! We've slept- never mind- but I know, Darius; she's the one."

He sighed and looked at me long and hard.

"Do you remember how you ended up here, Morgan?"

Thankfully, I didn't. It was something I had requested not to remember. I knew it was bad but I couldn't unlock that memory.

He eyed me darkly.

"Would you like me to tell you? You'll have no memory of it, just like you asked. It will be like I'm telling you a story."

"No. No I don't want to know. If I asked not to remember it must have been bad."

He shrugged but thankfully, let it be.

"So back to the matter at hand?" I pushed gently.

He sighed, long and hard.

"You understand that being human means suffering, a short life span and virtually no peace?"

I nodded.

I didn't know all that; as I said, I couldn't remember my last life.

"You realise what you're giving up for this woman?"

I nodded again.

"And you are completely sure of the consequences if this fails?"

I wanted to argue; to tell him that it wouldn't fail, we were in love, how could it fail?

I was willing to take what I considered to be not a risk at all.

He started at me for a long time, like was making up his mind before his eyes lightened and he nodded.

"Then it is done."

I blinked.

"It's done? That's it?"

He nodded.

"You're human now. Go be with her. Live your life as a mortal."

But he said it without any real joy in his voice, in fact, it almost sounded like a warning...

THREE

Life with Natasha was good. It was even better than I could ever have imagined; she finally came out to her parents, moved out and we got a place of our own. I even got a little part time job. It was perfect; better than I ever could have imagined.

I mean, sure we had our disagreements and things were a little heated and then went quiet for a week or so but that was completely normal...so I'd heard.

Every night, I prepared dinner for myself and Natasha and I made her a hot drink to help her sleep.

We were a proper couple. I loved her and she loved me, she'd never said it but she didn't need to, did she?

It showed in the things she did and the thoughtful ways she had.

Things were great, amazing even but as time went on, Natasha started to change and not for the better...

One night while I was making dinner, I heard the door open and close.

She was home.

"Hey Nat, how was work?" I called from the kitchen.

"Same as it always is." She muttered throwing her bag onto the couch.

She'd had a bad day.

I turned everything down so it wouldn't burn and went in to see her. I came up behind her and wrapped my arms around her waist.

"Bad day?" I asked, resting my chin on her shoulder.

"No, it was just boring."

"Well we'll have some dinner and watch a movie, that'll make you feel better." I suggested.

She shook her head tiredly as though she couldn't be bothered to answer.

"What's for dinner anyway?" She asked, her tone sharp.

She'd been like this for a few weeks now.

I thought maybe she was going through a phase or something or maybe she'd heard from her parents. They hadn't taken it too well when they found out their daughter was gay.

"Lasagna." I answered, knowing it was her favourite.

She sighed.

"Yeah, cause' we haven't had that this week already." She said sarcastically.

I frowned as she stepped out of my hold and turned around.

"You love lasagna."

"Yeah but that doesn't mean I want it every day."

"Stop exaggerating, we haven't had it every day, it was once." I said with a teasing note to my voice.

She sat down heavily on the couch.

"I'm not hungry anyway."

I watched her as she sat back, her eyes glued to the TV but she wasn't really watching it.

"Are you sure there's nothing wrong?"

She suddenly looked up at me and those eyes that I loved so much suddenly looked accusing and dark.

"How close are you and Lisa?"

Lisa was my co-worker and friend. We got along well. She had made me feel welcome the first day I'd started at the factory and she had helped me learn the ropes. We clicked from day one.

I shrugged as I sat down next to her.

"We're friends." I replied.

She gave me a side long look.

"She likes you, you know. I've seen the way she acts around you. I'm not blind."

"Well I don't see her like that and she knows I'm with you so..."

"And you think that's ever stopped anyone before?" She snapped.

I blinked.

"Nat, where is all this coming from?"

"I've been thinking."

I sat down next to her, taking her hand in mine.

"Hey, listen, I love you, Nat. Ok? Only you. I gave up immortality for you. There is no one else I would do that for. I swear."

She stared at me and her eyes were cold.

"I wondered how long that would take you." She said, her voice like ice.

I frowned slightly, not understanding where she was going with this. "What?"

"You blame me for what you had to give up."

"What? Nat that's insane. I chose to do this and I don't regret it, not for a second. I love you."

I repeated.

She stayed quiet and I sat back, looking at her. I frowned at her, realsing something;

"Why...why do you never say it back?"

Her jaw tightened but she didn't look at me.

"What?" She snapped.

"You've never once told me you love me but you do...don't you?" I hated the way my voice shook at the question; like I knew the asnwer and was afraid of hearing it.

She still wouldn't look at me. I licked my lips nervously.

"Nat?"

"What, Morgan?! For fuck's sake, what do you want from me?!"

"Tell me you love me." I said quietly, my eyes filling with tears.

She sighed and raked her black hair back.

"Why?"

"B-because I need to hear you say it."

"I can't." She muttered.

I frowned.

"Why?"

She turned on me then, her eyes wide and wild, her expression full of rage.

"Because I don't, alright?!"

My heart squeezed painfully inside my chest, the tears refused to fall and I just felt...numb.

She didn't...but then how could we...? Why...?

So many questions and none of them had answers.

I loved someone who didn't love me...

"Then...then what are we even doing?" I whispered.

She sighed and got up.

"I'm going to bed."

No. Not yet. Not untill she explained why we were living together, sharing a bed, creating a life when there was no love in it. It just didn't make sense to me.

I reached out for her,

"Nat, wait. Let's talk about this."

"I'm done talking tonight." She muttered, evading me.

I fell from the couch and got my feet, going after her.

"Nat, I need-"

"I said no!" She then turned and lashed out.

Pain hit me harder than I'd ever felt it. It stung my cheek and sizzled like I'd been burnt.

My lips felt wet and as I brought a hand to the corner of my mouth I realised I was bleeding.

She...she hit me?

She looked at me, anger in her eyes.

"I said I'm done talking."

I watched her go up to bed.

There was remorse, no sign that she was sorry for lashing out, nothing.

She admitted she didn't love me and now she'd hit me.

What had I done?

The next morning, I went into our bedroom, which I hadn't slept in that night- with a cup of coffee.

I sat down on the edge of the bed and Natasha rolled over, opening her eyes and looking up at me.

She eyed the cup of coffee I held and gestured to the beside table.

"Put that down." She said, her voice full of sleep.

I did and then she took my hand, stroking the back of it with her thumb.

"I'm so sorry I hurt you." She said, her eyes filling with tears.

I felt so relieved. She was sorry. She had empathy. She didn't mean to hurt me.

I gave her a small smile.

"It's ok, you had a bad day and you got a little...angry."

She nodded then let go of my hand to cup my now bruised cheek, running her thumb gently over my swollen lip.

"I should never have let it get that far, Morgan. I am so, so sorry."

I took her hand and kissed her palm.

"It's alright. It's forgotten."

She let out a breath and then sat up, resting back against the headboard.

I handed her the coffee.

"Thank you." She said and took a small sip. She smacked her lips together and winced.

I chuckled a little.

"Too hot?"

"A little." She said as she set the mug down again with a little laugh.

"Hey, it's my day off today. Want to do something?"

I smiled and nodded.

"Yeah, sure. What did you have in mind?"

"Well I was thinking we could go shopping. I could buy you something pretty, make up for last night?"

"You don't have to, Nat."

"I really do. I've always been so against hitting women and then-then I go and do it."

I didn't say anything, I didn't know what to say.

"Please, let me do this for you."

I gave her a warm smile.

"Ok but I'm buying us lunch out."

She rolled her eyes.

"If you insist."

So we went shopping. Natasha drove and I sat in the passenger seat feeling pretty good. It was summer so I wore big sunglasses to cover the bruise that was getting darker, just under my eye. The split lip, I covered that up with make up as best I could but if anyone said anything, I'd just say I fell over.

We went to the shopping centre and spent most of the day shopping. It was great fun; we went into all different kinds of shops and spent probably too much money but we were having fun; making up for a shitty day.

Something lurked in the back of my mind though; she had said she didn't love me...but then just like when she hit me, she didn't mean it so maybe she didn't mean that she didn't love me either. I nodded to myself, satisfied with that conclusion but then why was I still thnking about it three hours later when we were standing in line ordering our lunch?

We sat down with our plates across from each other and that thought still nagged at me. Maybe I should ask, clear the air completely.

"Nat, can I ask you something?"

"Sure." She said brightly as she stabbed her drink cap with her straw. "Bloody paper straws, worst thing they could've done." She muttered as it bent.

"Last night-"

"I thought that was forgotten." She said, a little snappishly.

I swallowed.

"It is but when you said you didn't love me...were you just angry? Did you mean it?"

Her features softened and once again, I felt that rush of relief.

She reached out across the table and took my hand.

"Of course I didn't mean it, Morgan. As you said, I was angry. I never want to hurt you again, you know that, right?"

I nodded.

I really did. I really believed she would never ever hurt me again.

A voice came into my head, female and warm, soothing-

"If they do it once, they'll do it again."

I frowned.

Who was that?

Natasha had a look of concern on her face.

"You ok?"

I nodded but I was still frowning.

"Yeah...I think."

That seemed to be enough to satisfy her and she popped a chip into her mouth.

I looked around the shopping center, watching all the couples mainly and seeing if there seemed to be any difference between them and me and Natasha.

I must have been deep in thought because Natasha sat back and let out a breath.

"Well that filled a hole. You ready to shop some more?"

Honestly? I was ready to go home. I couldn't get the voice or the warning out of my mind but I forced a smile and nodded.

I followed her around the shopping center for another two hours and she bought a few things. It was...pleasant. We didn't argue, she hadn't snapped at me anymore and I felt a little more relaxed.

She paid the car park attendant and then we went to her car where she threw the shopping bags into the boot.

I went to open the passenger door when she placed a hand on my arm. I flinched involuntarily and a sad look came over her untill she forced it back and plastered a smile onto her lips instead.

"You almost forgot."

I arched an eyebrow at her.

Had I forgotten something? Was it bad? But she was smiling so that meant it was ok, right? She wouldn't be smiling if it waasn't good. My mind whirled between good and bad. *Maybe this was a trap; maybe she was smiling because she was about to remind me that I had forgotten to do something and then she'd turn nasty again. What if she hit me? No. She said she wouldn't, she-*

"Morgan?"

Her voice brought me back and I blinked.

"Y-yeah?"

She held up a medium sized jewellery box, it was dark red and velvet.

"Here."

I smiled, feeling relieved and took it.

"No. Let me."

I gave it back to her and she opened the box to reveal a necklace. It was a little chunky but I liked that and the pendant was a heart shaped lock. Stainless steel. Beautiful.

"Nat...I-I love it."

"Come here. Let me put it on you."

She then pulled the velvet cushion from the box and produced a key. I blinked. This was interesting.

She spoke as she unlocked the pendant;

"You see, the pendant its self is the clasp and you unlock the clasp by unlocking the pendant, pretty cool, eh?"

I nodded as she took the other end of the chain, secured it to the pendant and locked the chain into place.

"Perfect." She said as she took a step back to admire the pendant resting against my chest.

"The best part of this- cause' I know you like all this touchy-feely crap- is that I keep the key and the necklace can only be taken off by me; so it's like I literally hold the key to your heart."

Why did that make me feel more like I was being owned and not shown love like I supposed she thought she was?

I kept the smile on my face even though I was beginning to feel uneasy.

She pocketed the key and I know it was probably just the way I was feeling but I felt like the chain tightened around my neck.

I swallowed as she gave me a wink then got into the car.

Later that night while Nat and I were watching a film; my phone buzzed.

I picked it up and saw that the text was from Lisa. I smiled and read it; she was telling me about work and how boring it had been. I chuckled and Nat looked over at me.

"Who's that?"

"Oh it's just Lisa. She was telling me how work went today."

Nat's jaw clenched and her fist curled on my leg.

"Like you care." She muttered.

I didn't say anything as I put the phone down.

"Do you?" She asked.

I shrugged.

"No."

She nodded but there was a frown on her face.

My phone buzzed again.

LEFT ME ON READ? RUDE LOL XX

This time, Nat grabbed my phone out of my hand before I could stop her.

I watched with baited breath as she read it.

"She's flirting with you, you realise that, right?"

I tried to play it off.

"Nah, she's just messing."

"She's flirting, Morgan. Look at this; two kisses?"

"We're friends." I said defensively.

"Maybe I should end her a text of my own."

I watched in horror as Natasha started typing out a reply.

I sat up, moving towards her.

"W-what are you saying?"

"Telling her to stay the fuck away from my girl."

I made a grab for the phone and she held it up, out of my reach.

"Nat don't do that, please. Honestly, she's just kidding. We're friends. She doesn't like me like that and I don't like her that either. Please, Nat, let it go."

She lowered her arm but still kept it out of reach as she turned that icy glare onto me.

"You seem pretty desparate for me not to text her. You sure something's not going on with you two?"

"No! Nat I love you! I've said all this before!"

For fuck's sake, what did I have to do to prove to this woman that I loved her above anyone else?

She then held the phone out to me.

"Tell her not to text you anymore."

I looked down at the phone and then at her again.

"What? I can't do that."

"Why not? It'll be no big loss if you lose her as a 'friend', will it?"

"Nat, this is crazy-"

That was when she hurled my phone at the wall and I watched as it smashed.

"Nat!"

"Nah fuck you! You're hiding something!" She raged as she got up. I got up too.

I didn't want to have this fight on the couch where she could look down at me and make me feel smaller than I already felt.

"I am not hiding anything! My god, Nat! What is wrong with you! Why can't you trust me?!"

She whirled around.

"It's her I don't trust!" She shouted, pointing at my broken phone.

"Then trust me! I would never cheat on you. I love you too much." I knew my voice was shaking, that I was on the verge of tears but I didn't want to keep fighting. I just wanted Nat to realise how wrong she was.

She looked at the ground and shook her head.

"I'm going to bed."

No...not this again.

"We can't just run away when things get hard, Nat." I snapped.

"Do I look like I'm running? I'm going to fucking bed." She snarled.

"We need to talk about this. We can't just keep being angry at each other. We need to sort this out."

"You wanna sort it, do you?"

I swallowed and nodded, taking a step back when she came towards me.

"Fine. Quit."

I blinked.

"Wh-"

"Quit your job, lose Lisa's number, break all contact with her."

"Nat, that's-"

"You can't do it can you?"

"Would you break contact with your friends if I asked you too?" I challenged; couldn't help it, my anger was getting the better of me.

"That's different. My friends are just friends."

"So is Lisa!"

"No, Lisa is a flirt who is pushing her luck."

I bit my tongue. I knew I was going to say something I'd come to regret but I could feel it bubbling up inside of me and maybe I shouldn't have but I goaded her into saying what I wanted so that I could throw this back at her;

"Yeah, cause' your friends never do that, do they?" I sneered.

"Watch your mouth, Morgan."

"Oh come on, Nat! We all know Tim wants to fuck you.!"

She came towards me, her eyes full of anger.

"We've been friends for years!"

"Yeah, I've heard how you and your 'friendships' work."

She lashed out. Again.

I fell to my knees as her slap sent me reeling. Once again, I was tasting blood.

She dropped to her own knees beside me instantly.

"Baby, I'm-I'm so sorry-"

I shied away from her and she didn't try to reach out for me, thankfully.

I licked my lips, tasting copper and my feeling my head throbbing.

If they do it once, they'll do it again.

That warning came back clear as crystal.

"Morgan, I'm sor-"

I crawled towards the couch, away from her.

"Don't...don't touch me."

I used to the couch to pull myself up and I sat on it.

She had done it again...

She'd hit me.

She'd promised she wouldn't do it again.

But she had...

I looked up and saw Natasha standing there with tears in her eyes but the strange thing was?

I didn't feel anything. Not a damn thing.

"Morgan? Say something-anything." She sobbed.

I stared at the window. It was dark outside and the rain was lightly tapping against the glass. The flat was silent, the film having long since ended.

I swallowed and brought my hand up to my mouth to wipe the rest of the blood away.

"I think I'm done." I said calmly; more calmly than I had ever done before.

"What?"

I sniffed and turned my head to look at her.

"I'm done, Nat."

"Done? What do you mean done?"

I looked around the flat. Everything in here chosen by her; her colours, her things, her pictures. This wans't our place; it was her's and I was just living in it.

I got up and headed for the stairs.

"Where are you going?" She called after me.

"To pack my things. I'll be gone in the morning."

She followed me upstairs and for once I wasn't scared about her lashing out or anything. I just wanted to get my stuff and go.

She came in behind me when I went into her bedroom and grabbed a bag, throwing it on the bed.

"I said I'm sorry, Morgan. You don't have to leave."

"No. I really do."

I opened the wardrobe and started taking my jumpers and jackets out, folding them and putting them in the duffel bag.

"I thought you said you love me." Nat said, her voice quivering but I could hear the anger behind it.

"I do."

"Then why are you leaving?"

"Because I'm done. I'm tired."

"So get some sleep. We'll talk about it in the morning."

I shook my head as I continued packing.

"There's nothing more to talk about."

"You said you wanted to sort this, let's sort it."

I sighed and stopped packing for a moment to look at her standing in the doorway.

"You said you'd never hurt me again...you did and you'll do it again."

"No, no I won't I promise-"

"Don't make promises you can't keep, Nat."

"Ok fine...maybe-maybe I need counselling or something but I don't want to lose you, Morgan."

I felt tears behind my eyes but my anger had started a war with my sadness.

"You think this is what I wanted?! I love you, Nat! I was building a life with you! A human life! But you're an abuser...and you always will be and I am tired of being the one who gives and gives and gives...I can't do it anymore."

I began packing again.

"You don't have to cut ties with Lisa."

"I know I don't." I muttered.

"I'll cut ties my friends, Tim! The one you don't like, I'll end it."

"No you won't. You'll tell me you will and then you'll call or text them behind my back. I don't want you to cut ties with any of your friends anyway, Nat; even if I hate them. I accept them because you love them...well as close to love as you can get."

She narrowed her eyes a little at that comment but kept begging anyway.

Eventually, her words all blurred together and I ended up not listening.

Once the duffel bag was packed I went to leave the bedroom but she blocked the doorway.

"I can't let you leave me."

"So I'm your prisoner now?"

"You don't want to leave...not really."

"I have to and you have to let me go."

She shook her head and her posture changed. She was on the defensive. I could get hit again here but I'd b damned if I was going to let her make me stay somewhere I didn't feel safe.

"Get out of my way, Nat."

"No. I can't."

"I want to leave and I am going to."

"You try to leave and I'll-"

"You'll what? You'll hit me again?"

I dropped the duffel bag from my shoulder and looked up at her.

"Go on then! Fucking hit me! You controlling, self serving, manipulative cunt!"

Her fist raised and I waited.

But she held it there, in my mid air.

"No, come on, don't hold back on me now. Fucking do it!" I roared in her face and she let loose...

It wasn't just one hit this time. It didn't stop and by the time it was all over, I was laying on the floor in a crumpled heap and Natasha was gone...

This was all new to me and I didn't understand why someone who was meant to love me, would hurt me the way that she did.

But then...she'd never said she loved me, had she?

My fingers trembled as I dialed Lisa's number. She was always kind to me and had a calming influence and I needed that right now more than anything.

I just hoped that she had a day off today.

I sat there, the phone ringing and ringing and tears fell down my face as I realised how truly alone I was.

There was a time when I thought Natasha would be all I'd ever need. I didn't need anyone else as long as I had her but now, even with her as my partner, I'd never felt more alone in my life.

Finally, she answered.

"Morgan?"

"Lisa? Hi- hi... I'm sorry to call you so early or if you've just gotten up but I...I was wondering if I could come over? I-I need to talk to you."

There was a pause and then concern filled her voice.

"It's fine, Morgan, really. What's happened?"

My voice broke and I cried all over again.

"Morgan, talk to me. What's happened?" She asked again but this time her voice held some measure of alarm.

When I was able to just about control my voice, I told her;

"It's Natasha...she-she hit me."

"She *hit* you? That's it, I'm coming round."

"No! No, don't do that. She's not here anyway. Can I come to you? Please? I don't want to make things any worse. I just need to be away from here-away from her. I don't want to be here when she comes back."

Lisa's voice softened.

"Ok-I mean, yeah of course you can. Do you need me to come and get you?"

I shook my head and sniffed.

"No it's fine. I'll be there soon."

"Ok and Morgan, if she comes back, say whatever you have to but just get out of there."

I nodded.

"Ok, I'll see you soon."

I hung up and got ready quickly.

I just wanted to be out of the house and with someone safe.

Lisa held out a cup of coffee to me as I sat on her couch, curled up underneath a blanket she'd draped across my lap.

She gently turned my face this way and that to inspect the damage. "She's given you a shiner and a split lip, take a week maybe to heal." She muttered.

I just shrugged. I didn't want to go into the fact that my ribs were sore and my back hurt. Maybe she had continued to beat me when I'd passed out...I didn't want to think about it.

She sat down next to me and frowned, deep in thought.

"What made her hit you?"

I swallowed, feeling embarrassed to even say it but I had to; she'd asked.

"She thinks there's something going on between us." I answered with an eye roll even as I felt my cheeks redden.

She grinned a little.

"I should be so lucky."

I gave her a look and she smiled.

"I'm only joking. She should know we're just friends."

I nodded.

"That's what I tried to tell her but she wouldn't have it. And...there's something else,"

"Go on." She urged gently.

"This might sound silly but whenever I said I loved her...she would never say it back."

Lisa frowned.

"That's not right. You should always say it back if you feel it."

I nodded in agreement.

"Yeah...that's what I thought."

Lisa reached over and held my free hand as we watched the TV which had the sound turned down so low you could hardly hear it but just her calming presence was enough.

"Lisa?"

She looked over at me.

"Hm?"

I licked my lips, feeling a little nervous.

"I know we're friends but if you had feelings for me-"

"I do." She cut in.

My lips parted in shock.

"What?"

She shrugged.

"I do have feelings for you but you're with Nat so I was just happy being your friend."

I swallowed. I had not been expecting that revelation.

"Ok, we'll...shelve that for a minute."

She gave me a sad smile but nodded that she understood.

"So, not to make this weird or anything but if...if I felt the same as you and tolf you I loved you, would you-"

"-say it back?" She supplied.

I nodded.

She gave me such a warm smile that even though I was in love with Natasha, despite all she'd done, it made me wish that I was in love with Lisa instead of her.

"Of course I would and I wouldn't hesitate. I'd keep telling you it as many times as you needed to hear it because if I knew that you were happy with me, that's all I'd ever want."

We stared at each other for a long while. I'd never noticed how deep her eyes were or how they were more of a light honey colour than just brown, and her dark blonde hair was wavy and long but had streaks of white blonde. She had a lovely smile and before I knew what was happening, we'd both met in the middle of the couch and were kissing.

It was so different with her; with Natasha it felt rushed, like she was scared we'd be caught but with Lisa, it was gentle, unhurried, like she wanted the moment to last for as long as possible.

When we pulled back, I stood and looked down at her, holding out my hand.

She took it and stood with me.

She knew what I wanted.

After sleeping in a cold bed with Natasha, I wanted to be with someone who wanted to show me that they loved me in every way. I believed with everything I had that Lisa would do that.

"Are you sure?" She asked carefully.

I nodded.

"What about Natasha?"

"We're over. I'm never going back."

She looked up a little nervously.

"Morgan, we don't have to this if you don't want to and I'm not just saying that because I know I have to but because I want you to be sure that this is what you want." She assured me.

Why couldn't she be the one I'd fallen for? The one I'd given up my immortality for?

"I want to." I told her , my voice a whisper.

We went upstairs to her room and she lead me inside, shutting the door quietly behind us.

She watched me as she pulled her top over her head and then slowly undressed me, leaving me standing there in my undewear.

"You're so beautiful..." She murmured before kissing me lightly on the shoulder.

I had a flashback to the first time that Natasha and I had slept together.

She had said the same thing.

I kissed her full on the mouth and then pulled back to look her in the eyes.

She held my upper arms gently.

"And this is definitely what you want?" She asked again.

I nodded and bit my lip as I felt new tears spring to my eyes.

"Morgan, we honestly don't have to-"

"No I do." I said quickly, afraid that she'd convince me to change my mind.

"Are you sure?"

I nodded and gripped the back of her neck.

"Just...just make me forget about her." I said, my voice shaking and tears blurring my vision.

She nodded, lifted me into her arms and carried me over to the bed...

The cool breeze blowing through the open window woke me.

I knew I wasn't at home. I wasn't in my own bed and that wasn't Natasha who was lying next to me.

I turned slightly and found Lisa with her eyes open, watching me.

I gave her a small, hesitant smile.

"How long have you been awake?" I asked softly.

"About an hour."

"And you've just been watching me?"

She nodded, a contented smile on her face.

I suddenly felt guilty and I sighed a little.

"Listen, Lisa. You know that this..."

"-it doesn't mean anything, I know." She said gently.

There was no anger in her voice, no malice. She just understood. Plain and simple.

She wrapped an arm around me, pulling me closer and looked into my eyes.

"So if it means nothing and this won't happen again, then can't I just treasure the time that I do have with you?"

I felt like crying again.

Lisa made me feel loved. She made me feel special, desired and wanted.

Why didn't I feel the way for her, the way that she felt for me?

I sat up slowly and she sat up with me, letting her arm fall away before she started wrapping the sheet around me so I could cover myself. It was a sweet gesture and I swallowed the lump in my throat.

She frowned, her expression one of concern.

"What's wrong?"

I turned around slightly and pressed a hand to her cheek, running my thumb over her jaw.

"Why can't she be you?" I whispered.

She smiled and shrugged, taking my hand from her face and kissing it.

"She's not that lucky."

She chuckled after she said it. Lisa was modest and the only time she would compliment herself was when she was joking.

"I should er - I should be getting home." I told her as I moved to grab my clothes.

"You're going back to her?"

I nodded.

"To say goodbye."

She blinked.

"You're ending it?"

Again I nodded; determined but sad all at the same time.

"I have to. I can't be with someone like that. That's not love. You showed me what love is supposed to feel like. I don't...I don't feel like that with her. I wish I did but I don't."

She nodded in agreement.

"If you need a place to stay, you can stay here- as a friend- I don't expect a...well you know."

I gave her a grateful smile.

"Thank you, Lisa I think I will be taking you up on that offer."

She smiled kindly and then left me to get dressed.

I knew she'd be there and when I let myself in later that morning.

I found her sitting on the couch, her face stoic but her eyes still held that gleam of anger.

She was still mad and if I didn't end this quickly, she'd try to hit me again.

I was sure of it.

"Where have you been?" She muttered, looking at her nails.

"Out."

"I can see that. Where?" She snapped.

I swallowed.

"I don't think that's any of your business anymore."

She frowned and looked up at me.

"None of my business? I am your girlfriend."

"You haven't been acting like it." I muttered, hanging my coat up in the hall.

"Because I hit you?"

"And the rest."

She let out a breath and got to her feet, brushing her hair back.

"Can we talk?" She asked, hands in the back pockets of her ripped jeans.

"I have nothing to say to you. Not anymore." I told her, my own anger flaring.

"So we're just going to carry on fighting?"

"No." I breathed and then looked at her as I prepared myself for her reaction as to what I was about to say.

"Natasha... I can't do this anymore."

She stared at me.

"Do what?"

"This. Us. It's...it doesn't feel right anymore."

"You're breaking up with me? Not just leaving like you threatened to last night? This is...final?"

I watched as the anger came through with each word and I stood my ground even though I was scared that she'd hurt me again. Not because of the pain I would feel but because if she did it again, I'm pretty sure I'd hurt her back and I didn't want that. I never wanted that and yet...I was about to. Maybe not physically but still, it would hurt.

She might not love me in the way that Lisa did and it wouldn't hurt her to hear what I'd done but it would defintely hurt her ego and that, she protected above everything else.

I finally nodded, making up my mind.

"I slept with Lisa last night. That's where I've been." I admitted, feeling a little ashamed.

Her eyes widened and she took a step towards me.

"You-you cheated on me?"

I nodded.

"I did."

I felt sad and ashamed but she needed to know the truth.

"You said you'd never cheat. You said that no one deserved to get cheated on and now suddenly that's all changed?"

"I never thought I'd ever cheat on you, Natasha but don't you see? Something has to be wrong for someone to be able to drive another to go against their beliefs and do it anyway. We're not good for each other or more accurately...you're not good for me." I added carefully.

She came towards me then, anger flaring bright as a flame.

I clenched my teeth.

I had somewhere to go.

I had someone that wanted to take care of me.

It didn't matter if she hit me.

At the end of all this, she'd have no one and I could walk away.

"Come on then! Do it! Hit me! Beat me again! It's the only thing you know, isn't it?!"

She paused in front of me but I couldn't help goading her.

"Why are you hesitating? We both know you want to hit me. You want to control me and now that's slipping you finally get it, don't you? You have *nothing*."

"You gave up immortality for me...you love me." She said, her tone soft but her voice quivered in disbelief; almost as though she was trying to wrap her head around the idea of what I'd actually done.

"But you don't love me." I countered, knowing it was true.

She grinned coldly but there was no emotion behind it.

"Your feelings are too strong. You wouldn't stop loving me just like that."

I nodded in agreement.

"You're right but I know what I need to do and Natasha, I don't want to be with you anymore. I do love you but I'll get over it."

I then went upstairs and continued packing what was left from the night before.

I heard the front door open and then shut and then she was gone.

I had my bag on my shoulder and picked up the other two as I walked to Lisa's.

I knew I wouldn't be there forever but it would be nice to stay with a friend until I figured out what I was supposed to do.

Natasha and I had bought the place together so we were both entitled to half of it but my stupid Angel brain seemed to remain with me and I decided that she needed somewhere to stay.

She would know I would leave it for her anyway.

I turned into an alley and found it blocked.

I frowned.

I was sure that this alley would take me into Lisa's street.

A white glow materalized before me and I stared in shock as Darius, one of the Arch Angels appeared in front of me.

"Darius, what are you doing here?"

"I have come to see you, Morgan. We have been watching and we know what has happened."

I nodded and hung my head.

"It wasn't-it didn't work out the way I had hoped." I admitted.

Darius nodded his head.

"I'm here to deliver punishment." He told me.

"There's no need for that, Darius. Yes, she hit me but we're over...I gave up my life as an Angel and it was a mistake." I said sadly, because I knew there was no way I could ever go back.

"I'm not here to punish her. I'm here to punish you."

I stared at him and wondered if I'd heard him right.

"Me?"

"You commited a sin. You were unfaithful."

I frowned.

"All mortals commit sins."

"Yes but not all mortals are Angels."

"I gave that up."

"Not entirely. You see, Morgan, you could never truly give up being an Angel because you have died once already. Yes, we took your powers, yes, you couldn't see your white aura or your wings but your soul? That is pure Angel and Angels..." He trailed off, letting the horror of what I'd done, sink in.

"Can't commit sins...not even one." I finished for him.

I knew the punishment for commiting a sin as an Angel and I panicked.

"I know what I did was wrong, I admit that but Darius, you can't do this, please! I'm begging you, I'll do anything!" I cried, dropping to my knees.

His jaw tightened as he stretched his hand out over my head and looked down at me.

"You belong to him now."

The ground started to shake and it opened up beneath me.

I screamed as I began my descent into Hell.

FOUR

Something was kicking me. Whatever it was had tiny feet and I wondered if it was a mouse.

I opened my eyes and my head started pounding.

I sat up slowly and brought my hand to my head. When I looked at my fingers, I found them stained with blood. I must have hit my head on the way down.

I looked up at the black cavernous ceiling and knew where I was.

The kicking continued until I looked down and saw a strange little blue pixie glaring up at me.

"Ah! There you are!" He said in his weird squeaky voice.

"What?"

"The master will be expecting you. Come on!" His tiny little clawed hand wrapped around a finger and with surprising strength, pulled me to my feet.

"Master?" I asked, my head still fuzzy.

"He will want to see you right away! We don't get many Angels down here! Oh, he'll be so happy!"

"I bet." I muttered as I let him pull me down halls and different corridors.

I sighed as he took a few more twists and turns and then stopped at a huge black door.

"Here we are!" He cried happily. *Too* happily.

"You know, I never thought I'd meet the devil."

He frowned up at me.

"And you never will! You're not that important!"

I blinked and looked down at him, his wings flapping so fast they looked like a blur.

"I don't understand."

"Behind this door is my master. Not THE master."

"Your master who...?"

"Turns Angels into Demons. That's his job. The devil wouldn't concern himself with something so trivial."

"Oh..."

Well that was one weight off my mind.

As an Angel we were told about the devil and all the horrors that he inflicted upon the evil and the sinners.

All of us never wanted to meet him after that so knowing that I would just be meeting an underling of his, that made things only a tiny bit better.

"In you go!" The blue pixie sang as he pushed me through the door.

I managed to stop myself just before I fell onto his desk.

The blue pixie's master looked like any normal human; small, slicked back hair and glasses. He looked like one of those uptown lawyers I used to watch when I was a proper Angel.

"Ah, Miss Morgan. Good to see you. Please, have a seat."

I sat down and looked around the office. I would have said it was nice had it not been placed in Hell.

"So you commited a sin and now you're here to become a Demon, correct?"

I nodded mutely.

We had all been talked to about this; the warnings and repercussions of sinning as an Angel. Descent into Hell- the demon modification- evil doing on Hell's behalf- then who knew what else.

"Any idea what kind you would like to be?"

"Prefferably one without horns."

He laughed loudly at that and then his expression turned serious as he regarded me.

"You've been hurt, haven't you, Morgan?"

I nodded, feeling suddenly very small and lost.

"Would you like to make her pay for what she did?"

I frowned.

"No. No I don't need her to suffer just because she hurt me."

He shrugged and then stood, walking-or more like pacing- up and down the office.

"Hm, I would have thought you would be more...vengeful but then you are-sorry-*were* an Angel so that might have something to do with it."

I watched him as he seemed to be thinking things through.

He then looked at me and it was an intense look.

"Still, you loved her. You gave up everything you'd ever known for her and how does she treat you? She hits you, accuses you of infidelity...she couldn't even tell you she loved you and then that's another question entirely, did she ever love you?"

Tears sprang to my eyes and I balled my fists.

"Stop it." I whispered.

"But it's true. You gave up immortality for someone who might not have even loved you."

"She did love me...she did."

"But she never said it...did she?"

I closed my eyes and forced myself to think back on every beautiful moment that Natasha and I had spent together. Of things she'd bought me, times shared where we'd laughed and she'd said nice things to me. It was the only thing I could do to stop myself from hating her.

"She never once uttered those three words that you longed to hear and don't you think that if someone sacrificed their power, they would deserve to know how much they were loved?"

"Maybe...but that-that just wasn't her. She couldn't help it." Even as I said it, I knew I was covering for her.

He shrugged.

"True, we can't help who we are but she hit you. She wanted to control you. She drove you to cheat on her...that just isn't you, Morgan... is it?"

"No."

"And she accused you of the very thing you ended up doing all because she hurt you that badly and I'm not just talking physical pain but emotional pain too. What kind of person does that make her?"

I felt my nails dig into my palms as I tried so hard to hold everything in.

He came to stand behind me and rested his hands on my shoulders.

"I mean, she's the reason you're here. If she had only told you how much she loved you or at the very least acted like she loved you, then maybe you wouldn't be here at all. Let's face it, she's the reason you have been punished. She's the reason you will become a Demon. She's the reason you never want to love again-

"I surged to my feet and spun around, knocking the chair back as I did and my eyes blazed with all the anger I'd ever felt since leaving Heaven.

"Alright! I hate her! Is that what you want to hear?! I hate that she's done this to me! I hate that she's the reason I'm not an Angel anymore! I hate that I was stupid enough to fall for a such a heartless, selfish, controlling excuse for a human being!"

He grinned at me as I breathed hard and my fists were clenched so tightly, I felt blood beneath my finger nails where I'd cut into the flesh.

"There. Now turn to the mirror, will you?" He said, calm as you like.

I did as he asked and he stood behind me, looking over my shoulder.

"What do you see?"

I shrugged.

"I don't know anymore..."

"I'll tell you what I see; I see a woman. Beautiful? Yes. Deadly? She could be. Would you like to see what I envision for you?"

I was scared but I had to know at the same time.

I nodded.

He grinned, snapped his fingers and I watched my reflection change.

My caramel coloured hair was longer and now jet black.

I seemed a little taller. My dress was now a corset-like top with a semi see-through, long flowing black skirt and killer high heels.

My make up was darker and I looked every inch the femme fatale that people are drawn to, only to find out that they've met their match and realised they have been seduced by someone they couldn't possibly handle.

I looked completely evil... and I loved it.

He grinned.

"What do you think?"

I looked at my reflection.

"I like it."

"Would you like to live like this? This could be your Demon form."

"Really?"

"Of course. Like I would make a beautiful creature like you into something hideous." He said, sounding only a little offended.

I looked back at my reflection and then nodded.

"Do it."

"Excellent! See you on the other side."

"Wait, what?"

There was a bright flash of light and then...I don't remember how I got there but when I woke up, I knew things would never be the same.

Ever again.

FIVE

"Miss?"

I turned my head and looked at the woman who currently held up two pairs of boots.

"Black or brown today?"

I frowned.

"Er...black?"

She smiled and put the brown boots back.

"Did you forget you had a riding lesson today?"

"Riding lesson?"

"You must have had quite a night last night, Miss. You don't seem aware of your surroundings."

My frown deepened as she came towards me and I placed a hand on her wrist.

"Sorry if I sound rude but who are you?"

She blinked and stared at me then offered a shaky smile.

"I am Sofia, your maid."

I have a maid...holy crap I have a maid!

"And er, how long have I been...wealthy?" I asked looking around at the luxurious space.

She chuckled.

"You were born into this, Morgan. It's all you've ever known. Do you want me to call a doctor?" She asked after a little while, a worried frown on her face.

"No, no it's fine. I should...I should probably get to my riding lesson." I said distractedly.

I walked past her to the door when she stopped me.

"Er, Miss?"

I turned back around to see she was still holding my boots.

I took them from her and slipped them on.

"Of course." I chuckled and zipped them up.

My house was more like a mansion with it's own grounds and I quickly learned that Sofia wasn't my only maid or servant. I had many and they all looked like they either respected or feared me. Had to say, I didn't hate it.

"Good morning, Miss. The trainer is waiting outside for you."

"Thank you, mr....?"

"Er it's George, Miss."

"George, right and how long have you been with us, George?"

He frowned a little at the question.

"Many years, Miss. I used to drive your father around."

I nodded, going along with it. I didn't even remember if I had a father. still, I must have done at some point.

If an Angel visited Earth and had to stay for longer to complete some quest or what have you, there was always a cover story, so it didn't surprise me that Demons also had them too.

"Of course you did. I had...a lot to drink last night. I must still be feeling the effects."

George nodded and gave me a warm smile.

"I understand. Would you like me to get you anything, Miss?"

"No, it's fine. I'll just...go off to my riding... lesson."

I tried to say it like it was the most normal thing in the world but obviously it wasn't and it would take some getting used to, this new lifestyle and everything that came with it but even as an Angel, I was a determined girl.

Outside, the sun was shining and birds were singing...I don't mean to make this sound idilic but it really was a lovely day.

I was pretty sure that just before I'd entered Hell it had been autumn. I looked at the ground, so rich and lush with green grass that was clearly looked after.

I looked around, searching for the trainer, expecting to see some stern, grey haired old man or woman with a stiff upper lip but that's not what I saw when I turned at the sound of hooves thudding on the grass.

Yes, she looked stern but she was about my age, which surprised me. She had white blonde hair that stopped just below her shoulders and as the sun hit her face, I saw shining ice blue eyes.

No trainer should be that attractive.

I swallowed and had to remind myself that I was a Demon. I was stronger, more powerful and I was attractive in my own right. I didn't need to feel intimidated by this woman.

I raised my chin and squared my shoulders.

She stopped the horse right in front of me so that I could feel it's breath on my face when I looked up.

"You're Morgan, I presume."

Haughty tone and she looked like she was literally on her high horse, except it was my horse and she'd do well to remember that.

"I am and you must be the trainer."

"My name is Chloe."

I only nodded that I'd heard her.

"You have ridden before, yes?"

I paused.

Had I? Was this part of my story? That I was an experienced rider? But if that were true, why would I need a trainer?

"Morgan?"

I blinked, realising I hadn't answered her.

"Once or twice, when I was a child."

She eyed me curiously and then nodded.

"Ok. So we'll start with the basics."

I watched as she jumped down from the saddle and held onto the reins.

She gave the horse a warm smile but when she looked at me, there was nothing but ice.

"Climb on then." She said, gesturing with her head to the saddle.

I walked up to the horse which now looked huge and gripped hold of the saddle as I started to pull myself up. I blushed when I realised that I couldn't pull myself up enough to actually climb into the saddle.

I heard Chloe sigh and then felt two strong hands on my thighs, pushing me up and I swung my leg over and was finally seated in the saddle.

"You were right, it has been a while since you've ridden."

My mind went somewhere else and I closed my eyes for a second to regain composure.

Stop it, you know she doesn't mean it like that. And why am I attracted to this woman who clearly doesn't like me?

When I opened them again, she was looking up at me.

"I think we'll start by walking first then maybe move onto cantering when you feel more confident. If you ever do." She muttered under her breath, thinking I couldn't hear her.

She made a clicking noise with her mouth and the horse moved forward as I dug my nails into the saddle and gripped with my thighs.

"Take the reins." She said and put them in my hands as we walked.

"Don't jerk on them, don't pull to either side or the horse will go whichever way you move, understand?"

I nodded.

She shook her head slightly and we walked on a little more, moving in a wide arc, away from the house.

"What's his name?" She asked suddenly.

"Who?"

"The horse." She sighed as though I were a child and she was bored by having to explain things to me.

"Oh erm...I-I don't know."

"Figures." She muttered with an eyeroll.

I frowned at her back.

"Ok, what is your problem?" I snapped.

She glanced back at me.

"My problem?"

"Yes. You haven't stopped snapping at me since you got here and I haven't been rude to you or anything."

She only shrugged but I was like a dog with a bone and I wouldn't let go.

"Have I said or done anything to make you dislike me?"

She looked back at me and stopped the horse.

"No."

"Then what is it?"

She sighed and patted the horse's neck as she looked at him.

"I'd rather you just be honest with me." I told her, keeping my tone simple and void of emotion. I didn't care about making her feel comfortable enough to talk and I sure as hell wasn't concerned about her feelings.

I'd made the mistake of putting another's feelings before my own once before and I wouldn't be doing it again.

She pursed her lips and then looked up at me. She looked like she was going to tear me off a strip but then her eyes seemed to lose their hard glare. She just looked...tired.

"I don't like women like you."

That caught me off guard.

"What?-"

"It's nothing personal." She said, shaking her head as if she wished she hadn't said anything.

"Nothing personal?"

"I'm sorry but you women are all the same; privillaged, work-shy princesses who don't really care about these horses. You only want to say that you know how to ride because let's face it, which rich girl do you know that can't ride a horse?"

"Is that what you think of me?" I asked, frowning slightly.

She nodded and then shrugged.

"You asked me to be honest."

"I did..."

"And now you don't like it so I guess we should be getting back and then you can fire me."

"Fire you?"

She nodded.

"I can't keep my feelings hidden for long, and once you rich girls find out how much I hate you all, I soon get fired. One even tried to run me down in her mercedes."

My eyes widened.

"Never!" I exclaimed in disbelief.

"True story, I promise you."

She let out a breath and took the reins from me.

"Come on then, let's get you back."

I reached down before she could lower her hands fully and touched her arm.

"Hey Chloe, I'm not going to fire you."

She frowned slightly, confusion written all over her face.

"You're not?"

"No. You're entitled to your own opinion and maybe as time goes by, you'll see I'm not like all those other rich girls." I added with a small grin.

She smiled back.

"No...maybe you're not."

She left once we went back to the house.

Sofia asked if I wanted anything and I shook my head, telling her I was going out for a walk.

She looked a little puzzled but then nodded.

I decided to walk up to the small town once I figured out where I was.

It was miles away from the town I'd come from but maybe this was what I needed; a new start, a new life...without Natasha.

I felt sad for a little while; thinking about all I'd lost and everything that I'd ever wanted had been snatched away from me but things were different. I couldn't wallow, and so I snapped myself out of it, thought about missing Lisa and felt sad all over again only...not so much.

When I looked up, I found that I'd reached the town and found a nice seating area surrounding a big square of green right in the center of the town itself.

I smiled to myself.

How the other half-and apparently now me-lived.

I started to walk over to one of the benches when I stopped.

There, sitting on the middle bench was Chloe, my horse trainer, and she was reading a book. I wouldn't have put her as the book reading type. I know you shouldn't judge but she seemed more like an 'all work and no play or relax' kind of girl.

I went to walk over to her when everyone and everything around me stopped moving.

It was like time had stopped.

I frowned.

Then in front of me, the blue pixie materialized from thin air.

"Hello Newling." He said, his voice similar to a buzz.

"Hello." I drawled back with a slight frown.

"I suppose you're wondering why I'm here and how time has stopped."

I nodded mutely.

"Well I am here to remind you that you are a Demon and you do have work to do."

I raised an eyebrow.

"Work?"

He nodded, his black eyes shining.

"Bad things. Make accidents happen. Try to buy a soul off someone. Anything in the name of evil!" He said with so much cheer I wondered what he would be like at a fun fair.

"Um....ok."

"Well, go on then. Get to it. The Master doesn't like to be kept waiting and he didn't give you this rich life because he likes you."

"He likes me?" I asked with a small smile that I tried and failed to hide.

The blue pixie rolled his eyes.

"Yes he likes you. He says you have great potential, whatever that means. Anyway, do something and do it fast. I don't like to keep coming up here. It's too...fresh and...airy." He said and shivered in disgust.

I bit back a grin and nodded.

"Fine. I'll do something... evil."

He nodded and smiled.

"Good. Hope I won't be seeing you again soon."

"Me either." I agreed.

With that, he was gone and time resumed.

I looked up and found Chloe still seated on the bench, too into her book to notice me standing there.

I turned and walked in the other direction.

I would start off small; I wouldn't try to excel on my first day as a Demon. I didn't even know how my powers worked or if I even had powers.

I found a trash can near an alley and decided to practice on that.

I checked that no one was around before I closed my eyes, envisioning a flame in my mind. I held out my hand, palm up and opened my eyes, seeing the flame dance in my hand.

I smiled and thrust my hand towards the trash can.

It lit up and I watched as it burned the contents inside to ash.

As I walked back, intent on finding something to light on fire as my first act of evil, I heard a couple arguing.

Rounding the corner, I found a man holding a woman by the front of her t-shirt.

He was snarling in her face and calling her all sorts of things as she cried.

I glared at him and bared my teeth, instantly angry.

"Hey!"

He looked up and so did she.

"Let her go."

"This doesn't concern you." He spat at me.

"Not yet but it will do if you don't let her go."

"She needs to learn some respect."

The woman cried again and I flew at the man, knocking him to the ground. I kicked him in the ribs as I got to my feet once again.

He glared up at me and before he could get up, I crushed his favourite appendage with my boot.

He cried out and tried to move my boot off of him.

"Apologize to her." I commanded.

"Are you fucking crazy?!" He screamed.

"Maybe. It's subjective. Apologize or I'll do worse." I threatened.

He looked between me and the crying girl.

"I'm-I'm sorry." He muttered.

I pressed down harder, making him cry out again. It would be useless to him after this, I'd make sure of it.

"I didn't catch that. Try again."

"I'm sorry! Oh my God I'm sorry! Please, just let me go!"

I glanced at the girl.

"Are you satisfied with that apology?"

She nodded, tears still streaming down her face.

"Good. Now go find yourself a real man, not this pathetic excuse."

She ran away then and finally, I stepped off the man.

"Looks like you'll be needing to rest it for a few months. A break that bad...you won't be using it for quite some time. Have a nice day." I smiled sweetly at him before walking away.

Damn that felt good. Maybe this whole being evil thing would work out.

When I arrived back at my house, Sofia quickly ushered me into my bedroom and started throwing dresses at me. She was frantic and running about grabbing shoes and make up.
"Oh you are so late!" She panted.
"Am I missing something?"
"The gala?" She said, pausing to stare at me like she couldn't believe I'd forgotten.
"Gala?"
She nodded and resumed her rushing around.
"Gala for what?" I asked, following her into my on-suite bathroom.
"You are to give a speech in honour of your father's charity."
Damn me and my back story.
"Oh right! Yes, I completely forgot."
"I know and we are so late! Just pick a dress and I'll sort out your make up as quickly as I can."
I decided on a sleek black number and high heeled strappy shoes to match while my hair and make up were done by Sofia's clearly experienced hands.
She basically dragged me out to the waiting car, bundled me inside, told me to make my family proud and slammed the door.
The driver nodded to me and then drove into the city to some big museum type building.
"Have a goodnight, Miss. I'll be here at eleven pm as per your request."
I nodded with an uneasy smile.
I didn't even know I had requested a time but then I didn't know that I was supposed to attend a gala.
I turned and looked up at the building, swallowing my nerves and went inside.

I stopped at the door and turned back around.

No one would miss me if I just walked away.

Ok, so I was supposed to give a speech, so what? What did it matter? Like anyone actually came to these things to listen to the spoiled daughter talk up her absent father.

Rolling my eyes, I turned and walked down the steps, pleased that I'd made the decision to avoid an uncomfortable situation.

Time stopped (literally) and I sighed.

It was never going to be easy, was it?

The blue pixie flew in front of me.

"Ohhh no you don't."

I frowned at him.

"What's the big deal? It's just some gala."

"It's not just any gala! It's your father's charity gala!" He cried.

"Yeah, a father I don't have and don't even know or remember."

"The master will be very disappointed if you don't attend."

I raised an eyebrow.

"I don't know why he'd be so bothered."

The pixie clawed at his face and I bit back a laugh.

He was so cute when he was mad.

"Things happen for a reason. You are supposed to attend the gala because this is the path you have been put on and you need to follow it through, otherwise your life as a Demon will not run as smoothly as the master would like and if he's not happy, he will be looking for someone to punish...catch my meaning, Newling?"

I nodded slowly, the smirk from minutes ago, leaving my face.

"Go to the gala, got it."

"Make the speech."

I nodded, turned around and went back inside.

I looked around and wasn't surprised to find that I knew no one.

How the hell was I supposed to give a speech to god knows how many strangers?

I took a deep breath and made my way through the room; the very large...very intimidating room.

Suddenly, someone grabbed my arm and pulled me into a small circle of people.

"Oh you must tell us how the charity is doing!" Gushed the woman who had grabbed me.

I nodded and forced a smile onto my face.

"It's going...good-great! It's-it's going great. I'm...very pleased...with the work that....we are doing...to help." I said haltingly as I had no idea what the charity was actually for.

The people I was talking to seemed pleased by this and I smiled and kept nodding to whatever they were saying.

"Excuse me." I said eventually and they nodded as I made my escape.

Was there any way that I could just hurry this along and go home?

I spotted the bathroom and made a dash for it.

I locked myself in one of the cubicles and sat down on the toilet lid which was thankfully down (I really should've checked that before I sat down), putting my head in my hands as I tried to think of a way out of this.

A light but insistent knock came at the door and I glared at whoever it was on the other side.

"Er, it's occupied." I said, my voice dripping with the undercurrent that would have added 'you dumb fuck', if I'd been so forward.

Another knock.

"Are you deaf?" I snapped, getting up.

Another knock.

I grabbed the door and yanked it back, preparing to give the insistent woman on the other side a real good talking to.

"Look I said-"

My sentence died on my tongue as I found myself face to face with Chloe.

She just smiled.

"Hi."

I couldn't help but smile back.

"You have no idea how pleased I am to see you!"

She gave me a puzzled look but the smile was still there.
"Really?"
I grabbed her wrist and pulled her into the stall with me.
"Oh ok, we're doing this." She said, stiffening a little.
I let go of her and blushed slightly.
"Sorry but...I have no idea why I'm here. I know none of these people. I'm supposed to give a speech and when I saw you, I just..." I trailed off, not knowing what to say.
"It's your father's charity gala. You have been raising millions for poor villages in Africa." She said with a look that said, 'why didn't I know this?'
"We have?"
She nodded.
"Wait...why are you here if you hate privillaged girls?" I asked, wondering why she had turned up looking like a goddess clothed in light pink silk, her hair and make up done to perfection.
She looked like a model.
She lowered her head slightly and I bit the inside of my cheek to keep from grinning.
Finally, she confessed.
"I heard you were going to be here." She said, her voice small.
I felt a bit more confident at that and raised my chin, my ego coming into play.
"Oh really?"
She then turned cold.
"Oh don't look so pleased. You said you wasn't like these other girls. I only came to see if it was true."
I raised an eyebrow.
"So you've been watching me?"
She squared up to me, refusing to let my arrogance intimidate her.
"I've been watching how you interact with guests and how you treat the staff...you don't treat them with the same contempt as the other girls."
I smirked and shrugged.

"Maybe because I wish I could take their place and they would have to make the speech that I wasn't prepared for."

She chuckled and her eyes brightened.

"Oh yes! The infamous speech by the daughter of the Hunter clan!" She exclaimed.

I closed my eyes, the humiliation of everything made crystal clear thanks to her.

"So this is an annual thing then?"

She nodded.

"Your sister used to do it before she moved half way across the world."

"That bitch." I muttered, wishing that she were here to save me from all this, whoever she was. I hated having a back story, especially one that I wasn't debriefed on.

Chloe suddenly took hold of my hand and pulled me out of the bathroom stall.

"Time to make your speech I think."

I pulled back as we neared the door.

"I can't."

She looked back at me and pulled again.

"You have to."

"I really can't. All those people... I just-no."

She sighed and then looked at me, her face an expression of complete seriousness.

"I'll make the speech with you."

"You will?"

She nodded.

I smiled gratefully at her and then wrapped her in a tight hug.

"Thank you."

She smiled and I felt her pat my back awkwardly.

"You're right..."

I pulled back to look at her.

"Right about what?"

"You really aren't like the other girls."

I grinned and nodded.

She smiled back and then straightened her shoulders, head held high. "Alright then, let's do this."

SIX

Chloe gave me an encouraging smile as she followed me onto the stage and then stood back, letting me take the floor.

I glanced back at her and she gave me a double thumbs up.

I could do this...bloody hell, I had to do this!

I licked my lips and watched as everyone in the room turned to look up at me, drinks in their hands and pleasant smiles on their faces.

Although some had clearly used too much botox and I couldn't tell if they were smiling or if the injections had left them that way.

Pushing the thought aside, I started with my speech.

"Thank you all for coming. I know my father would have been proud to see so many of you supporting his vision tonight."

I swallowed as it hit me.

I'm a liar.

I didn't know my father from this life and I didn't know what charity work he'd done, if any. I was a Demon now so why would charity work be involved if I was a being of evil?

None of it made sense.

I heard Chloe clear her throat and I brought myself back to the moment.

Just finish the speech and then you and her can get out of here. Me-I meant just me-
I could get out of here.
"I know he would be overwhelmed by seeing so many of you here and I just wanted to say thank you for that and I hope we all continue to help this charity to grow and give these kids a second chance-"
I was just about to finish my speech with a 'thank you' when I stopped.
It couldn't be...
My eyes suddenly felt like they were stinging and I wanted more than anything to run from the building.
Finish the speech. Panic later! My brain hissed.
"Uh...yeah, so thank you. Goodnight."
I turned and fled the stage, Chloe following close behind me.
Once again, I found myself in the bathroom stall, trying to breathe deeply and control my racing pulse.
Chloe crouched down in front of me, her hands on my knees.
"What happened out there? You freaked!"
I nodded but I couldn't speak.
"Did you get stage fright?" She asked, searching my face for any sign that would clue her in as to why I acted like I had.
I looked into her eyes and realised that she didn't need to know and besides, I couldn't tell her.
It wouldn't matter to her and I didn't want the first person I'd found myself actually liking, knowing that I had been the victim of domestic abuse.
"Morgan?" She pushed gently.
Finally, I swallowed and nodded.
"Yeah...something like that."
She stood and held out her hand.
"Come on, let's grab a drink."
"Actually, Chloe, I just...I just want to go home."
She nodded in understanding but I saw the brief look of hurt flash in her eyes.

"It's nothing to do with you. You're right, I did freak during the speech but..." I paused, bit my lip.

What to tell her?

How much should I tell her?

The bare minimum. As I said, she didn't need to know.

"But what?"

"I-I saw my ex. That was all."

She paused, holding my gaze, searching my eyes. I didn't know what she was looking for though.

"Your ex." She repeated slowly.

I nodded.

"I looked out at the audience and she was just...there. It's like she's here to get noticed. She's the only one wearing a red dress." I said with a roll of my eyes.

"So she'll still be out there then, won't she?"

I nodded, biting my lip again.

"Do you want to see her?"

I frowned as though the question offended me.

"What? No! No of course I don't."

Didn't I?

Didn't I want the chance to show Natasha that I'd become someone? That I was rich now?

I could go out there with Chloe on my arm, pretend she was my girlfriend just for tonight.

I'm sure she'd agree if I asked her.

I shook my head.

Fantasies, that's all they were.

"Maybe we can slip out the back?" Chloe suggested, dragging me away from my thoughts.

"Do you think we could?"

She lifted one shoulder and then grinned.

"We could try."

I nodded and she took my hand again.

"There's normally an exit through the kitchens." She whispered as we crept out of the bathroom.

We were just about to move when Chloe stopped and dropped my hand instantly.

"What is it?"

She nodded in the direction of where her eyes were glued.

I was still grinning, thinking she was trying to play a trick on me or something.

I turned my head and my smile dropped quickly.

Natasha.

I straightened and Chloe suddenly peeled away. I watched her disappear into the crowd.

Why did she go?

I pushed the thought aside as Natasha walked over to me.

She was dressed in a clinging red dress that showed off her back and nude coloured high heels with her jet black hair in a slightly different style than to what she normally had but then I looked different too; black hair instead of brown, more dark princess than fallen Angel now.

"Morgan." She said, looking me up and down but she had a small smile on her face, not like the anger I was used to seeing.

"Hi." Was all I said, was all I could say.

"You look good." She said.

"Thanks. You too."

Natasha looked over my shoulder in the direction Chloe had gone.

"Who's the girl?"

I frowned, annoyed at the forwardness of the question.

She hadn't changed; always wanting to know things that she had no business knowing.

"Does it matter?"

She gave a small shrug.

"It's just a question."

I narrowed my eyes at her.

"You know it's never just a question with you."

She sighed and rolled her eyes and I turned to walk away muttering, "I'm leaving."

"Wait."

I turned back as I felt her hand on my wrist.

"Get. Off me." I snarled, remembering the last time she'd laid a hand on me.

She instantly backed up and held her hands up to show me she wasn't going to hurt me.

"I'm not that person anymore, Morgan. I've changed."

"People like you don't change, Natasha. No matter how much you want them to."

"I have! So have you, obviously." She said, looking me over once again.

Why did it feel wrong when she did that now?

At one time, I would have given anything for her to look at me like that again, like she used to when we'd first met but now...now I wanted to run and I wanted to find Chloe.

That was my out.

"I should go and find Chloe."

"Oh, so she does have a name."

Her voice dripped with sarcasm and I clenched my teeth, steeling myself as I turned away from her.

"You moved on quickly."

I whirled around, anger getting the best of me.

"I'm not with her and even if I was, it has nothing to do with you, not anymore."

Natasha's eyes grew cold and I knew what was coming.

I licked my lips, just waiting.

She moved close to me so that she was only an inch or two away and I stayed exactly where I was, willing myself not to turn and run but to face her and whatever cruel words may come out of her mouth.

"You think getting over me will be easy? Just because you've found some blonde thing to take your mind off me?"

I stayed quiet, knowing she wasn't done as she rested a hand on my shoulder and lightly dug her nails in.

It didn't hurt but she knew that I knew it meant she was showing her possessive side.

"You can go out with as many girls as you like, Morgan. You can sleep with as many as you need to but we both know that I'm the one you want to come back to and if you're a good girl...maybe I'll let you."

I felt tears behind my eyes and I clenched my teeth as those same tears fell.

"I will never want to come back to you." I said, my voice shaking.

She chuckled darkly.

"You can keep saying it but it doesn't make me believe it anymore than you do.

You wouldn't be crying if you didn't care."

I heard the smirk in her voice, saw it when she moved to look into my eyes.

"Do you even care how much you hurt me? How you broke my heart after I gave you everything I had? Gave up everything I'd ever known? Do you care about anything but yourself?" I practically sobbed.

She didn't say anything but that arrogant smirk stayed on her face as I continued to cry, tears falling silently to the floor.

"I loved you...and you abused that. I'm done with you." I snarled.

I walked away then but Natasha always had to have the last word.

"Over my dead body you are."

I stopped as a cold feeling went through me. I didn't recognize it and I shook it off, frowning as I continued walking through the crowd.

It was high time I found Chloe.

I found her sitting by the fountain in the museum's gardens.

She looked up at me and frowned.

"Shit, you look terrible, what happened?"

I just shrugged but the truth was that I felt broken all over again.

"Nothing."

"It doesn't look like nothing."

"Do I look that bad?" I asked even though I didn't really care.

She shook her head.

"No...it's just...your eyes look-you look-I know this is going to sound strange but you look...broken."

I nodded, fighting back tears and bit my lip.

"I think I'd like to go home now." I whispered.

She nodded and put her arm around my shoulders as she walked with me around the front of the museum to the waiting car outside.

Must be 11 o clock...

Back at home, I curled up in a ball on the couch.

Chloe came in about ten minutes later with a mug of coffee.

"Sorry it took me so long, you have a massive kitchen and way too many cupboards." She chuckled lightly.

I said nothing, didn't even smile as I took the mug from her and just held it, staying in my half fetal postion with a blanket draped over my legs.

Chloe sat down next to me and her voice softened.

"Do you want to talk about it?"

I shook my head.

"It might help."

"It won't." I muttered, feeling numb.

"Well we can talk about something else; the speech, the gala, the museum itself or-"

"She thinks I'll go back to her." I said, interuppting Chloe's rambling.

Chloe frowned, her blue eyes darkening.

"And will you?" She asked after a pause, her voice tight.

"No. I don't want to." I told her honestly.

"Then what's the problem?"

I closed my eyes and shook my head.

"She's too sure of me. She thinks that no matter what she does, I'll always be there."

"But you ended things with her." Chloe said with a confused frown.

"She thinks it's temporary."

"But it's not. Surely she must know that."

I shrugged.

"I don't think she does; I gave up...a lot for her." I said awkwardly. Obviously Chloe didn't know about my past or even what I really was. Part of me wanted to tell her and then the other part of me didn't because of my mistake with Natasha.

I fell too hard too fast.

"What did you give up?" She asked.

"My whole life. I changed everything to be with her."

"That's why she's so sure of you." Chloe realised.

I nodded.

"It's that more than anything that really angers me. If she wasn't so smug about it I could let it go but she is and she rubs my nose in it." I sat back and let out a breath.

"Sometimes I really want to make her pay."

Chloe went eerily quiet and I looked over at her to see that she was deep in thought.

After a little while, she turned slowly to look at me.

"So make her pay."

I stared at her, not sure if she was serious or not.

"What do you mean?"

"People like her are always getting away with treating people like dirt. She needs to know what she's done so that she doesn't do it again."

Her tone was so low and bordered on dangerous that I wondered if she was joking with me, seeing how far I'd go.

"I don't see how I can." I said flippantly.

"Not just you; us."

My eyes widened at her.

"Us? You mean you'd help me?"

She shrugged.

"Why not?"

"You're my horse trainer...why do you care so much?"

She shrugged again.

"Maybe because I like you and I think that in time, we could become friends. What do you think?" She asked with a coy smile that could almost be interpreted as flirting.

I smiled despite how heavy and numb I was feeling and nodded.

"I'd like that."

"Ok so now I'm your friend, I want to help you do this."

I raised an eyebrow at her.

"Really?"

"Really."

I gave her a warm smile.

"Then you're a good friend."

She returned my smile and gave me a little nudge.

"You want some ice cream?"

I nodded.

"Sounds good. Did you want to stay and watch some crappy movies with me whilst we eat this ice cream you speak of?" I asked, trying to make it sound as good an offer as I could.

She nodded.

"I would love that."

Maybe Chloe wasn't as straight laced as I'd once thought.

SEVEN

The next morning I woke to find myself alone.

I frowned a little at being left in my current state but then Sofia breezed through the door and gave me a bright smile.

"Good morning, Miss. Did you have a nice time at the gala last night?"

I nodded but then grimaced as memories of Natasha's cruel words came back to me.

Shaking my head, I asked instead;

"Where's Chloe?"

Sofia frowned in confusion.

"I didn't even know she was here."

"Yeah, she came back with me last night."

At Sofia's slightly shocked look, I explained myself.

"Not like that. We just watched movies and ate ice cream."

Sofia nodded that she understood but there was still an awkwardness there.

Surely my own staff knew what I was like and what or more accurately who, I preferred the company of.

I shook my head.

"It doesn't matter. Anyway-"

At that, the phone started to ring and Sofia rushed to answer it.

I frowned as I watched her cheerful disposition change to one of confusion.

"Uh...yes she's here."

I walked towards her as she held the phone out to me with a slight frown on her face.

"She's insisting on talking to you. She-she's very rude."

My heart started to race as I knew who was on the other end but it couldn't be...Natasha didn't have this number.

She wasn't apart of this life but then she had been at the gala, a place she had no right to be and my grip on the phone tightened as I put it to my ear.

"I know you're there." She said when I didn't say anything.

I swallowed and licked my lips, forcing myself to speak and finding that I couldn't.

"It's alright. I'll just talk and you can listen."

So I did.

And I didn't think she had the power to break me again but dammit that's exactly what she did; she told me how worthless I was. That it didn't matter that I'd changed my hair colour or style, I would always be the Angel that gave up everything because she thought it was all for true love, and then she went on to tell me that it didn't exist and that I had a choice to make; I could go back to her and we could try again or I could stay where I was and she would always be there; always reminding me that I had made the worst mistake of my life and that she was just out of reach, even when she knew I still wanted her. Maybe not in the way I once did but there was something still there and she could see it.

I was just about to hang up, feeling weak and drained when she said something so chilling, I froze on the spot.

She told me that she knew what Chloe did for a living and she knew where she lived, what route she like to walk in the mornings and that it would be all too easy to be rid of her.

Natasha wasn't a killer but she had her ways, and people I liked didn't stay for long so maybe it was a good thing that I was away from Lisa. I missed her, she was a good friend after all but at least she was safe this way.

When she hung up, I fell to the floor, feeling so very cold and numb. Sofia came rushing in and knelt down beside me.

"Morgan! Are you ok? Who was that?"

"An ex." I muttered.

She didn't say anything more, just moved me to the couch and said she'd make me a coffee.

I sat there, feeling trapped and there was something else simmering beneath the surface.

It didn't feel like anger...I didn't know what it was.

Sofia came back in with the coffee and handed it to me.

I thanked her and then asked for the phone.

Chloe picked up on the first ring.

"Morgan? You ok?"

"I need to see you. Now."

I sat there feeling on edge. I hated that feeling and when I heard the doorbell ring I flinched.

Sofia walked in followed by Chloe.

I gave her an uneasy smile and she returned it with a sympathetic one of her own.

"Hey...you ok?" She asked awkwardly as she sat down beside me.

Sofia turned and left the room with a warm smile, saying she would come back a bit later to see if we needed anything.

Chloe licked her lips, she was also sitting on the edge of the couch with me, her posture stiff.

"So are you going to tell me what's wrong?"

I looked at her and I knew by the look on her face that she could see the tears that were threatening to fall.

"I heard from Natasha." I began.

Chloe frowned slightly.

"Oh..."

"She knows about you. I don't know how but she does."

Chloe's frown deepend.

"Why does she need to know anything about me?"

I shrugged.

"She thinks we're together."

"But we're not."

"I know but she's like this; she thought I was having an affair with my co-worker when I wasn't- I mean I did- but not until she'd hurt me enough." I added.

Chloe seemed like she was deep in thought and then nodded like she'd come up with an idea.

"She would destroy your life if given the chance...wouldn't she?"

I nodded and then so did she; looking like she'd made her mind up.

"Leave it with me."

She stood and walked towards the door.

"Where are you going?"

"Just trust me." She said over her shoulder.

I heard the door shut and then total silence.

Just what was she up to?

I paced around all day and still hadn't heard anything from Chloe.

I just hoped that she hadn't gone and done anything stupid.

Sofia kept coming to check on me, offering me either coffee or tea, biscuits, crisps but I couldn't eat anything. I was too worried.

I finally went to sleep exhausted and when I woke the next morning, I still hadn't heard anything.

Sofia came and sat next to me, giving me a look of concern.

"Maybe you should call her." She suggested softly.

"I tried." I said quietly, biting the skin of my thumb.

"And she's not answering?"

I shook my head.

"No...her phone's off."

Sofia let out a small sigh.

"Do you know where she lives?"

I frowned as I thought about it.

She was my horse trainer. Maybe I had her address somewhere.

"Do we have her information?"

Sofia got up and went over to a desk in the corner, rifling through the drawers.

If we do, they'll be in here."

I waited, hoping that she would find something.

After a few minutes, she got up and held up an envelope in a show of triumph.

"I have it!"

I lept to my feet and went over to her.

"Well done, Sofia. I'll swing by her place and take a look."

She smiled, pleased that she'd helped.

I went to see where my chauffer was and asked if we could go to Chloe's house, just to check and see if everything was alright.

It turned out that she didn't live far and the house wasn't what I had imagined.

It was small and quaint but there was something dark about it, something I would never have paired with Chloe.

Yes she was guarded but she seemed pretty light and easy going, this house didn't resemble that at all.

I thanked my driver, got out and went up to the front door.

Hopefully she wouldn't be mad that I'd got her address and had turned up unannounced.

I knocked and waited.

Nothing.

I frowned.

I was sure she was in.

I heard a thump that sounded like it came from around the back. I was curious by nature anyway and so I went to check it out.

The lawn lead right to the back garden and I followed it until I came to a generous sized shed.

There was more noise and it was coming from inside.

Maybe she had a project?

I smiled to myself as I imagined her at a work bench, sawing or painting something. The girl was full of surprises.

I opened the shed door and stopped dead in my tracks.

I couldn't speak.

I didn't know what to say as I saw Chloe in a scene I thought I'd never see her in; there she was, a sharp looking knife in her hand as she stood in front of a chair and tied to that chair...was Natasha.

EIGHT

Chloe turned around, her ice blue eyes wide as she saw me standing there in shock.

"Morgan...you-you wasn't supposed to see this." She said as she turned, knife still in her hand and my gaze went straight to it.

She followed my gaze and saw the knife hanging limp in her hand. I now realised with horror that her white tank top was spotted with blood.

She stood in front of Natasha so I couldn't see if she was still alive.

"What...what have you done?" I asked, my voice a whisper as I felt like I couldn't breathe.

She glanced behind her and then down at the knife.

"I-I did it for you. Morgan, she was ruining your life, I had to do something!"

"By killing her?!" I cried, tears forming in my eyes *(some Demon I was)*.

"She's not dead." Chloe said and I almost missed the disappointment in her tone.

"She's not?"

Chloe shook her head and stepped back so I could see Natasha.

She wasn't dead. Just badly beaten.

"I wouldn't kill her...not without your permission." Chloe added in a small voice.

I turned back to face her.

"Why would I ever give you my permission to kill someone?"

Chloe frowned slightly as if she was confused.

"Because you're a Demon, aren't you?"

I felt my like my heart had stopped for a second.

"How do you..."

"How do I know?" Chloe finished for me, a small smirk on her face.

I swallowed and waited for her to explain.

She rolled those blue eyes of her's and started circling Natasha who was just barely holding onto conciousness.

"You think it's coincidence that I just happened to turn up as your horse trainer? You think that someone like me would ever want to train someone like you? No darling, I'm not a horse trainer. I am the Master's shall we say, Enforcer?"

I frowned.

"Enforcer?"

She nodded.

"I make sure that wayward Demons stay on the path set for them."

My frown deepened.

"You think that your mission in life is to commit evil acts in his name?" She questioned, tilting her head in askance.

I didn't respond.

"Oh no, baby...it's not like that."

She then pointed at Natasha.

"She is the reason you became a Demon and she is the reason that you're holding back. From life, from love, from everything! I'm just here to help you become something Hell can be proud of."

"So all this...it leads back to her?"

Chloe nodded.

"She's your first mistake and until you erase all proof of that, you'll never be free and thankfully, you gave me a way to help you."

She then stepped forward, holding the knife out to me.

"All you have to do is kill her and your life-your true life-can start."
I looked down at the knife she was holding out to me, her eyes imploring.
I shook my head slowly as my gaze never left the wicked looking blade.
"No...I won't do that."
I turned and ran out of the shed.
Seconds later, I heard Chloe following me.
I felt tears behind my eyes and I couldn't look at her. I didn't want her to see how upset I was.
"I don't see why you're getting so cut up about this, no pun intended." She added with a shrug.
I kept my back to her.
"I just can't kill someone."
"But it's not just someone. It's Natasha, the girl who made your life a living hell. She hurt you, used you and you're telling me you don't want to make her feel all the pain you felt?"
"I did once, sure but then... things changed."
"What changed?" and I could hear the confusion in her voice.
This time, I turned around and let her see the tears that had yet to fall.
"I met you and like an idiot I thought that you-" I cut myself off.
No. Never again.
"Thought that I what?" Chloe pushed.
I held up a hand to stop her.
"Nothing."
We both stood there in silence until she grinned at me.
"So what am I supposed to do with your ex girlfriend tied up in my shed?"
I shrugged.
"Let her go?"
"And she'll go running to the police and you'll be spending your life in jail. Yeah, great plan." She said with an eyeroll.
I frowned at her.

"You'll go down for this. Not me."

"Uh, I'm not earth bound. You are. I'm an Enforcer of Hell. You're just a Demon. A minion."

"I am not a fucking minion!" I shouted.

I don't know why out of everything this was the thing that made me angry and the fact that she was comparing me to one of those pill shaped yellow things angered me more than I can say.

She held the knife up again.

"Tell you what, come back, torture her for a bit, see how you like it and if you still don't want to kill her, I'll do it."

"So either way...Natasha dies?"

Chloe shrugged carelessly.

"Looks like."

In my stupid brain, I fought to make a plan.

Maybe if I went along with it long enough, I could buy Natasha some time until I figured out a way to get her out of this and maybe I could escape as well. Not with her but just...alone, somewhere.

I didn't even have a plan.

This was not going to be easy.

NINE

I was once an Angel.

I believed and served all that was good and pure and just, so tell me please, why I am sitting here in the rain, on the front steps of my mansion feeling nothing but hate, pain and anger?

I shook with the rage I felt.

All I could think about was what Natasha had done to me. The things she'd said and didn't say when I needed to hear them, how she'd beat me and threatened to do more than that if I ever brought up the subject of love again.

I raised my head to the thundering sky, it's colour mirroring my mood and the crack of lightning like a whip to match my anger.

She had broken me in ways I'd never experienced. She'd changed me into something I hated. I was a Demon because of her. Everything that had happened to me, all of it, was because of her.

My fists clenched as I rested them on the knees of my torn jeans.

I didn't believe in love anymore. It was just a fairytale told to children to help them believe that life wasn't full of pain and disappointment. It was something they could hold onto and look forward to because they were made to believe that love is all that matters when everything else is all going to shit.

What they don't tell you is how love can do more harm than good. They don't tell you that the one you open your heart to is the one who also has the power to break it and that sometimes they do it just to take pleasure in your misery.

Natasha deserved everything that Chloe wanted to do.

Being an Enforcer of Hell, she obviously knew all sorts of ways to torture her and prolong her pain but maybe I didn't want Chloe to do it.

Maybe I wanted to.

Maybe I needed to.

I stood slowly as the rain dripped off me and brushed my soaking hair back.

Sofia had known to leave me alone and now I walked in the rain back to Chloe's house.

The rain hadn't eased at all and I didn't bother going up to the house; Chloe wasn't the one I wanted to see.

I walked around the side, pushing on the door and letting myself into her back yard.

The shed stood there with it's doors shut, a sliding bolt in place but not locked.

I walked up to it and pulled the bolt back, feeling it slide free and I pulled the door open.

Chloe had been at work again.

Natasha looked up and her blue eyes squinted as the light came spilling in.

I shut the door behind me quietly.

Natasha had been gagged and there was a cut on her cheek, her nose looked like it had been bleeding and she had blood on her teal coloured tank top.

She was trying to talk to me but her voice was muffled and I couldn't understand her.

I stared down at her.

"I suppose you're asking me to help you now. I can't understand you through that thing but I've listened to you talk long enough, haven't I?"

She stopped trying to talk and frowned, tears drying on her face.

I pulled a chair out from the work bench and straddled it as I sat in front of her, my arms resting on the back of the plain chair.

We were face to face now and I brushed her hair back like I used to do when we were a couple.

"She's hurt you, hasn't she?" I asked, my tone soft, almost sympathetic.

She nodded and closed her eyes, when she opened them again, a tear slid free and dropped on the leg of her jeans. I watched it fall, feeling numb.

"Are you in pain, Natasha?" I asked.

She nodded, more tears falling.

"Does it hurt when she hits you?"

Again, another nod.

"Does it make you think about when you hit me?"

She looked at me, a frown on her face but she didn't nod.

I sighed like I was disappointed.

"It's a shame really. I thought that you being here, Chloe torturing you, it would make you realise what you'd done to me. But it hasn't, has it? You still think you're the one who's hard done by, don't you?"

She didn't nod or give any indication that she agreed but now she was looking at me with hatred in her eyes.

She'd worked out that I wasn't on her side anymore.

"I admit that when I found you here with Chloe, I was shocked. I didn't think it was right and that she should let you go but now...after everything and a lot of thinking things through, maybe this is exactly where you should be."

Tears welled up in her eyes again and I reached forward, wiping a stray tear from her cheek gently and she recoiled back from me.

"Oh baby, don't be like that. Don't cry. After all...you deserve this."

I sat back and she sagged against her restraints.

"So here's what's going to happen; I'm going to let Chloe do what she wants to you and each day I come here, I'm going to ask you a question. If you don't answer or if you give me the wrong answer, I let Chloe rough you up some more but if you say the right thing, I'll set you free. Sound fair, darling?"

She glared at me and I grinned.

"See you tomorrow."

I left the shed and slid the bolt back in place.

When I turned around, I found Chloe standing there, her arms folded and a cold smirk on her face.

"Thank god. I thought you'd gone soft." She said.

I rolled my eyes.

"I may have been a little hasty in what I said to you about letting her go."

I glanced back to the shed.

"She deserves this and I've been thinking about how she's made my life a living hell." I said, turning back to Chloe.

She nodded in agreement.

"So I want in. You torture her and I'll play a little game of my own."

Chloe grinned, showing perfect white teeth and nodded.

"Sounds fun."

"Oh it will be."

......

She held up well. I was suprised.

Chloe didn't let up, she didn't give her moment's rest. Every time I went up to that shed I could hear Chloe taunting her, I heard the wet smacks as Chloe slapped or hit her and I knew the wet sound was because of the fresh blood that had dripped down from open cuts. I sometimes stood outside, leaning against the door just listening.

I never heard Natasha beg before but she begged constantly now. She pleaded with Chloe to stop. She screamed, she cried and still Chloe didn't buckle. Not like I would have at one point in time.

As promised, I asked her the same question every day and every day she got it wrong or sometimes refused to answer, saying that there was no answer, I was just prolonging the torture and giving her a slice of hope to make the pain that much more worth it, knowing she'd never get the right answer.

What she didn't know was that there was a right answer but I knew she'd never get it.

One particular day, I caught Chloe just as she was coming out of the shed, wiping her bloody knuckles on a piece of rag.

She gave me a small smile but lately that smile had dimmed. She was tired and this game of torture wasn't fun anymore, it had become a neccessity and she knew that now I had started it, I couldn't give it up.

I guess you could say that I was on a kind of power trip.

"How's she doing?" I asked, my arms folded.

Chloe shrugged.

"She's not holding up so well anymore. She nearly blacks out after three hits."

I frowned and anger boiled inside me.

"She's playing you! What's the point in this if she's not even concious enough to feel it?!"

With eyes blazing, I strode past Chloe and into the shed, shutting and bolting the door behind me as I heard Chloe try to follow me.

"Morgan. Morgan, what are you doing? Let me in! Morgan!"

I ignored her as Natasha loked up at me, a gag in her mouth, her blue eyes hazy but full of hatred and loathing.

"It doesn't work that way, Nat. You're supposed to stay awake when Chloe's torturing you." My voice shook as I feared that my control was slipping.

I needed this control over Natasha. I needed to feel bigger than her, more powerful but I was the one close to the edge and not willing to let go or even pull myself back.

"Ok, question time!" I exclaimed, clapping my hands together.

I turned to face her.

"What is the one thing that you know about yourself that you can't handle?"

She looked like she was thinking but the end, she let her head hang forward and her shoulders shook as she sobbed.

I reached forward and ripped the gag from her mouth, letting it hang around her neck.

"Please...please, Morgan just let me go."

"That's not the answer we were looking for, Nat. Come on, think!"

"I don't know! You ask me every day and I don't know!" She cried, the sobbing becoming more pathetic by the minute.

"Just look inside yourself. Be honest for once in your fucking life!"

She shook her head and then slowly, as if she'd had another thought, raised it and glared at me.

"If you're going to kill me, just do it."

I crouched down, elbows resting on my knees as I came down to eye level with her.

"I don't want to kill you, Nat." I whispered, my voice soft.

She frowned but there was a glimmer of hope in her eyes.

I would enjoy crushing that.

"You don't?"

I shook my head, allowing a small, warm smile to play across my lips.

"No. I want you to suffer, and if I killed you, you would be free, so no, I don't want you dead, Nat. I want to keep you around just a little while longer."

The hope in her eyes faded and I stood up again, looking down at her as I pushed the gag roughly back into her mouth again.

"We'll try again tomorrow. Really think about the answer, Nat. Remember, if you get it right, I let you go." She looked like she didn't believe me and she shook her head to show me as much.

"I still keep my word when I promise something. The fact that I'm now a cold hearted bitch is all down to you, and you may hate what I've become but the truth is that the bitch I am now? You created her. Deal with it."

I turned and unbolted the shed, stepping outside and finding Chloe sitting on the back porch, a sour look on her face.

I smiled at her and she didn't return it.

"What's the matter with you?" I asked as I walked up and sat beside her.

"This can't go on forever. Sooner or later you're going to have to kill her and let Hell have her soul." I frowned.

"I don't see why. She has yet to answer my question."

"But there's no right answer is there? You're just toying with her." Chloe said, sounding disgusted.

I turned to glare at her.

"Wasn't it you who wanted this? Wasn't it you who pushed this? And now suddenly it upsets you?"

Chloe sighed and raked her blonde hair back.

"I'm an enforcer of Hell. I make sure that it's Demons follow the rules and you're not following them."

I shrugged.

"I'm just softening her up a little."

It was a lie and she knew it.

Quicker than I could blink, she pulled a hunting knife from her boot and held it up against my neck, gritting her teeth at me.

"Finish her or I finish *you*."

I just laughed at her and she pressed the blade a little deeper into my skin. Anymore pressure and she would draw blood.

"Go on then, do it."

She blinked and I felt the pressure ease but only very slightly.

"What?"

"I said do it. Press down. End it."

She licked her lips and I saw tears spring to her eyes.

"I can't..."

"Why?" I barked.

The knife fell away and I grabbed her hand, forcing the knife back to my throat.

"No. Come on. You're an enforcer of Hell! Do your job, Chloe!"

"I can't!" She wailed and threw the knife away, putting her head in her hands.

"I can't kill you..." She whispered brokenly.

I knew why. She knew why. I wasn't sure when or how it had happened but after spending all these weeks together, something had changed within our dynamic. Chloe had stopped becoming someone who worked for Hell to make me stay in line and instead, she had decided to ally herself with me, but I knew I had to put a stop to it before it got out of hand.

"Nothing can happen." I told her, my voice firm.

She nodded but then frowned and looked at me.

"Why can't it?"

"Because I'm not someone who can be loved and I sure as hell can't love back."

She nodded as she glared at the shed, almost as if she could see Natasha and was glaring at her.

"You can-you could- at one time but she ruined that."

She then turned to look at me and hesitantly she took my hand. When I looked at her, her blue eyes were pleading, almost innocent.

"Maybe-maybe you could learn to-"

"No. I can't." I snapped, taking my hand back.

She grew angry then and she got to her feet.

"You think I want to feel this way about you?! I hated you! I wanted nothing to do with you! And now this! I know you feel something too, you just won't admit it!"

I got my feet too.

"Because there's nothing to admit to, Chloe!"

"So you're telling me that if I said I'd take you to bed right now, you wouldn't follow?"

"Is that what you're saying?" I challenged.

Our eyes locked and she grabbed my hand, tugging me towards the house.

"Wanna find out?"

I lunged forward and pushed her up against the wall of the house, attacking her neck with my teeth and tongue.

She moaned, fisting her hands in my hair and raking my scalp with her nails. I then plunged my tongue deep inside her mouth and I groaned as she bit down on my bottom lip.

I spun us around and pushed her so that she was facing the wall. Kicking her legs apart I slid my hand down the front of her ripped jeans, finding her warm and wet.

I kissed the back of her neck and she arched against me as my other hand wrapped around her waist as I teased her with my other hand.

She whimpered and I could feel her heart beating wildly.

"Oh god, just get on with it." she growled.

I grinned against her neck and chuckled darkly.

"Beg me." I whispered, licking the shell of her ear.

"I don't beg." She snarled.

I then cupped her, letting her feel my fingers dangerously close to where she wanted them.

"You will."

"Is that a promise?"

I nodded and bit down on her pulse point.

She let out a low moan and tried to grind down on my fingers.

"I want...I need..."

"Yes?"

She bit her lip and I knew she was close to begging.

It was then that the heavens opened and the rain fell, soaking us both.

"All you have to do is tell me what you want." I whispered in her ear.

"You mean beg you." She said, annoyance in her voice.

I grinned.

"One moment of weakness for many of pleasure." I promised.

She groaned as I toyed with her, giving her a little taste of what was to come if she did as I asked.

"Oh god...ok, ok, Morgan, fuck me, please!"

I grinned and the smirk remained in place as I plunged two fingers deep inside her. She cried out in pleasure and arched against me, her hips thrusting to meet my fingers as I curled them inside her.

"Oh fuck...fuck, Morgan..."

"Is this doing it for you?" I teased.

She groaned.

"Oh god, you know it is."

I moved my fingers faster and harder and I kissed the side of her neck.

She wound her fingers in my hair to keep my head there as I rubbed against her, trying to relieve my own mounting pressure and letting her hear my harsh breaths mixing with her own.

"Oh, oh fuck, Morgan. I'm gonna...I'm gonna-"

I grinned and bit lightly at the sensitive skin on her neck.

"Come for me, baby."

She cried out as pleasure over took her and I picked up the pace, my fingers moving fast and hard. She followed my movements, screaming at me to go harder and faster still. I did until she went boneless and sagged back against me.

I let out a breath and removed my fingers from her jeans as she turned around in my arms.

"That was..."

I smiled and her eyelids fluttered like she was falling asleep while leaning back against the house, the rain had slowed a little.

But then she recovered quickly and grabbed my hand, pulling me towards her.

"That must have gotten you pretty hot yourself."

I nodded.

"That it did. Watching you get off...knowing it was me making you feel that way, Natasha never made me feel that desired."

Chloe moved closer to me and gave me a gentle kiss.

"She didn't know how to love you." She said softly.

I raised an eyebrow, my guard still up, protecting my icy heart.

"And you do?"

"Let me show you."

I stayed where I was.

"We're still talking about sex, right?"

She chuckled and nodded.

I gave her wink.

"Then I guess I would like you to show me."

She grinned.

"I was hoping you'd say that."

TEN

I got dressed quickly, trying not to wake Chloe as I zipped up my boots and raked my tousled hair back.

I heard her stir and glanced over my shoulder to see her eyes opening slowly.

She smiled at me and then frowned when she saw that I was dressed.

"Where are you going?" She asked, her voice sleep tinged.

"Home."

"Home?"

I nodded and stood, sucking in a breath, knowing what was coming. She sat up slowly.

"Do you have to?"

"Chloe, you knew this wasn't-"

She held up a hand to stop me.

"I know. I just-I just thought that maybe...maybe after what we did, you'd-I don't know- feel

differently...about me?"

I bit my lip.

How to let her down gently but firmly?

"Look, Chloe, last night, it was great. I had a great time but-but that's all it was. I can't love again. I've told you that. I'm not saying it to be cruel, I'm saying it so that you can get on with your life."

She looked down and I hated seeing the dejected expression on her face.

"I'm sorry...I don't want to hurt you but-"

She threw back the covers and swung her legs over the side, grabbing her clothes.

"It's fine. I get it."

Her voice was hard and I knew she didn't get it, she didn't understand.

"Chloe-"

She spun around, hand up to silence me again.

"Morgan, I don't need to hear it, okay? We had fun, it was one night. That's it. Now didn't you say you were going home?"

I nodded my head slowly.

"I'm going to check on Natasha first." My voice was small.

She shrugged.

"Whatever."

She went into the bathroom and slammed the door.

I went downstairs, grabbed a bottle of water and went out to the shed.

Cracking open the door, I found Natasha slumped over.

She was asleep.

I tapped her shoulder and she woke with a start, breathing heavily through the gag. When she looked up and saw it was me, the hate returned to her eyes.

I held up the water.

"You need to drink."

She shook her head, looking away.

"Natasha...come on."

She ignored me so I reached down and roughly pulled the gag down from her mouth. She let out a breath but didn't say anything.

I unscrewed the cap and crouched down in front of her.

"Are you going to drink for me?" I asked.

She glared at me but then after licking her dry lips, she nodded.

I gave her a small smile and tipped the water bottle near her mouth and watched as she gulped great mouthfuls of it. She then glanced at me as she was drinking and I knew she was done.

As I was putting the cap back on, she looked at me and suddenly spat some water she'd been holding in her mouth straight into my face.

I closed my eyes and calmly wiped my face with my free hand.

"I can make Chloe go easy on you, you know. Just answer my question."

"You and your fucking question." She snarled.

I shrugged.

"Just answer it."

She glared at me.

"What is the one thing that you know about yourself that you can't handle?" I asked, reminding her of the question I asked her every day for what had almost been a month now.

She looked at me and I could see that most of the fight had left her eyes.

"Who I am...that's what I can't handle." She said, her voice so soft I didn't know if she'd even spoken at all.

I licked my lips.

"And who are you?"

She sighed.

"I'm cruel, heartless, vindictive and...I hate myself."

I sat up a little straighter.

"Do you regret what you did to me?"

She nodded and she looked up at me.

"Being here, it's given me a lot of time to think and I know what I did to you...it was wrong."

I felt tears behind my eyes and I swallowed the lump in my throat.

"Do you mean that?"

She nodded and tears welled up in her own eyes.

"I do...Morgan, I-I'm so sorry."

I'd never seen her cry before and I held back my own tears.

I didn't feel any anger towards her. I didn't hate her. I felt some kind of...relief?

I put a hand on her shoulder.

"I forgive you, Natasha."

I meant it. I really did.

She gave me a small, broken smile.

"I'm going to talk to Chloe and see if we can get you out of here."

She frowned in confusion.

"Why can't you let me go?"

I winced.

"It's a long story and besides, I need to be respectful to Chloe. We made this decision together after all."

Natasha sucked in a breath and nodded that she understood.

I got up and moved to the door but I looked back at her over my shoulder.

"I'll come back. I promise."

She smiled that small smile again.

"I know. I trust you."

I went back inside the house and found Chloe sitting in her arm chair by the window, reading a book.

She didn't look up as I walked in.

"She answered the question." I said.

"Good. So can we kill her now?" She asked, turning a page in the book she was reading.

I frowned.

"No. I made her a promise; answer the question, we let her go."

This time, she did look up and then shrugged.

"Oh...well that's disappointing but ok, if that's what you want."

I nodded.

"It is."

"Fine."

She stood and put the book away, going to the door.

"Wait, that's it?"

"Well the sooner we get rid of Natasha-I mean- let her go, the sooner they'll put me on some other job and that means I'll be far, far away from you."

I frowned at her back as she brushed past me.

"Chloe, I didn't mean to hurt you."

"You didn't but I also realise that I don't want to be around you anymore. I want to go back to Hell and be an enforcer to some big name and make a name for myself instead of dealing with these...small time revenge gigs. It's boring."

I nodded but I didn't believe her.

She was hurt and I was the cause of it but she was going to let Natasha go so I guessed that the best way to deal with this was just to go along with what Chloe wanted.

Chloe turned as she shrugged on her jacket.

"Call your driver. Tell him to meet you out front and I'll bring Natasha out."

I nodded and went to do just that.

I waited for the car to pull up and less than fifteen minutes later, it rolled to a stop beside me.

Turning on my heel, I went through the side gate to the shed.

Pulling open the door to announce to Chloe and Natasha that the car was here, I stopped in the doorway and my heart nearly stopped.

Natasha was gone. So was Chloe.

Chloe had played me.

Why was I suprised?

ELEVEN

I ran back out to the car and jumped in the back.

"Chloe's gone and she's taken Natasha!"

The driver, James, seemed calm but he knew what to do and sped away, going to god knows where.

I sat in the back, feeling scared, angry and unsure.

I didn't know what to do or where to go. Where could Chloe have taken Natasha in that short amount of time?

Then my phone started to ring and I answered it quickly, knowing it was Chloe.

"What the hell have you done with her?!"

"She's fine. I don't know why you're so angry, Morgan."

"You bring her back! Right now!"

"Why? What do you think is going to happen here, Morgan? That you and Natasha will go back to being lovers?"

I paused.

"Friends maybe?" She pushed.

I didn't know what to say but I had a horrible feeling that she knew something I didn't.

"Oh baby, haven't you figured it out yet? Natasha can't love you. In fact, she can't love anyone! Isn't that right, Natasha?"

I couldn't hear her so Chloe spoke for her.

"She's a little busy right now but while I've got you on the phone, I'll tell you one thing; You and Natasha meeting each other was no accident. Nothing ever is. Come to the address I'll give you and I'll tell you everything you need to know."

.....

Twenty minutes later, I was in some abandoned downtown street with boarded up houses.

No one ever met at swanky hotels or nice bars anymore, did they?

I walked into the address of the house she'd given me and looked around.

There was no sign of Natasha or Chloe.

I walked further into the dark room.

Wallpaper was peeling from the walls and the floor was rough hardboard. There was no lighting, only from the cracks that were coming through the boards from outside.

"Chloe?"

At the mention of her name, she appeared from around a doorway.

A cold grin plastered on her face.

"I knew you'd come."

"I said I would, didn't I?" I snapped.

She just stared and then moved towards me; started circling me like a bloody lion eyeing up it's kill.

"You came here for her."

I swallowed, not wanting to admit that was true so I raised my chin and clenched my teeth to maintain some sort of control.

"You said you'd tell me everything."

She nodded, still circling me.

"I did."

"So talk." I barked and she flinched away a little.

A look of irritation came over her face and she sighed.

Finally, she stopped circling me.

"Do you remember how you would watch Natasha for days on end when you were an Angel? You were praying you'd never get caught. You didn't even work your way up because you were afraid that the person they would assign you to wouldn't be her."

I frowned.

I knew my own history, why was she repeating it back to me?

"She was everything to you, wasn't she? You would sell your own soul if it meant that she was safe. The truth, my dear Morgan... is that she already did."

My frown deepened, creasing my brow even more.

"You mean-"

"She hasn't got a soul. She sold it. Years before you even knew she existed."

"Why-why would she do that?"

Chloe shrugged.

"Why does anyone do anything? Because they want more and she was no different."

"What did she want?"

Chloe grinned, showing off her perfect white teeth.

"She wanted you. Well, not you exactly, but she asked for someone who would love her completely for who and what she is. She had no idea that they would send her an Angel.

When she met you, she knew you were what she sold her soul for but as time went on, she was so sure that the love you had for her would never die or diminish that she abused it, she abused you. She didn't know that you would leave her.

She thought she'd sold her soul for you-for someone like you- and therefore you were bound to her. Here's the catch; she said she wanted someone to love her and accept her, she didn't specify that they were to stay with her forever so naturally, Hell found a loophole and they brought you in.

An Angel becoming a Demon? That gives Hell some major points."

"So Natasha and I...we were just pawns in a power struggle?"

Chloe nodded after a moment's thought.

"Sort of. I was brought in once they saw that Natasha was back in your life-this current life. They knew that there was a chance you could go back to her because as I said, Natasha asked for someone to love her and she got what she asked for; you will always love her. Maybe not in the way you used to but there's still something there, and I think you know that."

I frowned, hating to admit that Chloe was right. I didn't love Natasha the way I used to but I still cared.

"So where is she?" I asked with a shrug.

"She's safe for now but you, you're a Demon and if you think you can run away with one of the damned, you are very much mistaken."

"I don't want to run away with her. The time for me and Natasha has passed but you're right, I do still care about her. I care about what happens to her. So I want her to live her life, away from all this."

Chloe shook her head and chuckled darkly.

"She doesn't have a life! She's damned! She did it herself and she has to accept it."

"No. There has to be another way. She sold her soul and she shouldn't have."

"Her soul belongs to Hell now, there's nothing you can do to change that. Just...just let her go." Chloe sighed, sounding bored.

"I-I can't."

"You have to. You and her, you're different people. You are a Demon and she is Hell's property."

I wrinkled my nose in disgust at that.

"No one owns anybody."

"Hell does." Chloe shot back smartly.

I turned away from Chloe raking my hair back and feeling lost and hopeless.

"I want to see her."

My voice was breaking and tears threatened at the the feeling that I was powerless, that there was nothing I could do.

Chloe sighed.

"You can't."

"Why not?"

"I was commanded to send her to Hell. They don't tell me why, they just give out the orders." Chloe explained with a shrug.

"Then I need you to take me to her."

Chloe frowned.

"No. It doesn't work that way."

She then moved towards me and gave me a shy smile.

"Look, why don't you just forget about Natasha? What if you and me-we became something? A Demon and Hell's Enforcer? Imagine how powerful we'd be. You can't deny how good we are together and you don't love Natasha anymore."

I nodded in agreement,

"You're right, I don't. But I don't love you either."

"You could."

"I'm not doing this again, Chloe, so you take me to Natasha or I'll-"

"You'll what? What can you actually do, Morgan? You have no real power. You're not in any position to order me around, you have nothing and no one."

She was right...

Chloe sighed once more and then turned and walked out, tossing a comment at me over her shoulder.

"Think about it and get back to me. Once you see that saving Natasha isn't an option, you'll come around."

I went back home but there was no one there.

Sofia, the rest of the house staff, all gone. Hell must have been informed of what I'd tried to do.

The house was dark, clouds formed overhead and the house itself was cold, like no one lived there.

I walked into the lounge and sat down on the marble floor, the icy chill of it seeping into my bones.

I looked up at the ceiling and started thinking about all the Angels up there; Darius, the other Arch Angels; were any of them watching me now?

Tears slid down my face and I cried.

I started voicing my thoughts.

I admitted to all the wrong I'd done, all the mistakes I'd made, everything from watching Natasha and no one else, to falling for her and giving up my life as an Angel and how I'd do anything to take it all back.

Nothing was worth this.

I silently promised that I'd be better. I'd do better and I was wrong to put my faith in something so evil.

Time stopped and I clenched my teeth. That little shit of a pixie was about to show himself.

Sure enough, he did.

"Have you come to scold me?" I bit out.

He said nothing, only looked at me.

"Well? Come on then! Out with it!" I raged.

I looked into his black eyes and I saw something there.

He looked....sad.

"You failed."

I nodded, hanging my head.

"I know..."

"You failed as an Angel. You failed as a Demon. The Master doesn't like you anymore and Heaven will never accept you for what you have done."

Silent tears escaped my eyes and dripped onto the marble.

His tiny clawed fingers gently lifted my chin so that I looked at him.

"Yet...I like you."

I frowned at him.

"You do?"

He nodded and gave me a small broken smile.

"You tried to save someone who could never love you. You still saved a stranger from that abusive boyfriend even though as a

Demon you should have let it happen and walk away. Even after everything she's done, you still wanted to save Natasha. You still want to do the right thing even when you were made into a being of pure evil. That means that it doesn't matter who owns your soul, your path in life will always be one of the good."

I listened intently, mainly because I needed to hear something that made me sound like I was at least trying to do the right thing.

I was doomed, damned, whatever you wanted to call it so why not hear a little something good about myself before Hell called me back. What was the harm in that?

The pixie still looked into my eyes, that sad smile still there, his tiny claws holding my chin.

"Maybe...maybe you deserve a second chance."

I didn't even have the strength to look hopeful. There was no hope anyway.

"Good luck finding someone that can make that happen." I said with a broken grin.

He stared at me.

"...I can."

I glared at him.

"Is this another cruel joke? Kick a girl when she's lower than she's ever been? If you're fucking with me, you can just quit while you're ahead."

"You forget that Pixies inhabit the Earth, Hell and sometimes if we're lucky, Heaven too. Their rules don't apply to us as we come from another realm anyway. A realm that no one has the power to touch but us, so yes... I can help you."

I wanted to believe him. I really did but I was so scared to hope.

I sniffed and licked my lips nervously.

"How?"

His smile brightened just a little.

"Close your eyes."

I was scared.

What if I opened them and I was here again? What if he was lying to me? What if I woke up in Hell?

"Trust me." His small voice whispered.

Trust a pixie? That was asking for trouble.

He rolled his eyes.

"Please?"

I took a breath and closed my eyes.

I felt his tiny claws on my forehead and then... that's it.

Nothing.

I didn't feel anything.

There was no blinding white light, the ground didn't open up and swallow me whole, nothing like that but when I opened my eyes, I was standing on a street corner of my hometown.

The sun was shining, people were walking about, shopping or having coffee, cars drove up and down, it was so...normal.

I jumped when the blue pixie materalised beside me, hovering.

"Jeez!"

"Relax, they can't see me. Only you can and only just this once before you start your second chance then you'll never see me again."

Why did that make me a little sad?

"So what has Hell got in store for me this time?"

He frowned and folded his arms, his eyes set on something across the road but all I could see was a park.

"It's not Hell. This is all my doing!"

"You?"

He nodded.

I let out a breath and folded my own arms, bracing myself for the worst.

"So what am I now then? What have you turned me into? A pixie like you?"

"You wish." He muttered.

"A harpy? A sphinx? A witch? Werewolf? Vampire maybe?"

He turned to look up at me and smiled.

"A human."

"A what?"

"A human."

"And-and what am I supposed to do as a human?" I asked.

"Live your life, Morgan. Live it as you wish. Heaven has no need of you and Hell doesn't own you. You are to live as a mortal and what you do on Earth now, that will determine what happens when you die, just like everyone else walking around now." He said, gesturing to the people around us.

I couldn't help but smile.

"You did this?"

He shrugged.

"Everyone needs a little help sometimes and you were dealt a cruel hand, Morgan. And who knows maybe now you're human, you'll get to right some of your wrongs." He said with a knowing smile.

He then looked back to the park and I saw her standing there.

Chloe.

"Is that...?"

"She doesn't know you in this life, Morgan."

"Maybe that's a good thing." I said sadly.

He nodded in agreement.

"No one is what they once were here, Morgan. This is your second chance and their's as well. Chloe is just like you now. A human."

I smiled, feeling happy and so relieved beyond words.

"Thank you. Thank you so much for this. I honestly thought there was no way out."

"Well now you know there is. Just don't mess this one up."

I nodded.

"I won't."

He smiled then.

"Have a good life, Morgan."

"Thanks and once again, thank you, for everything."

He nodded and then was gone.

I looked up caught Chloe's eye. She looked back at me briefly before she glared and turned her head away.

For just a second, she looked like she might know me.

Chloe- or at least the Chloe I knew- was bright, funny and a little stoic at times but even when I'd been a Demon, she was a good person deep down.

Natasha had been too before she'd sold her soul. I wondered if she was here somewhere too.

Pushing that thought aside for a bit, I headed across the road and went into a coffee shop. I just wanted to sit for a bit and think about what I was going to do next. Afterall, my life was my own once again.

The door opened again once I'd sat down with my coffee and rushed footsteps sounded on the floor.

"I'm so sorry I'm late! Bloody buses."

I looked up and saw Natasha hurrying through the coffee shop as she spoke to who I guessed was her boss.

"It's fine honey, but we're getting busy though so be down in five."

"Yeah, sure thing." She said and hurried out the back.

I smiled to myself.

There was Natasha, soul intact and everything.

As promised, Natasha came back down, ready to work and instantly she was sent out to take orders. She stopped at my table and looked down, seeing I already had a coffee. She went to move on but her eyes caught mine and she smiled.

I knew that smile.

It meant she was interested in what she was looking at and for just a moment, my heart did a happy little flip.

"I can see you already have a coffee but would you like something to go with it? A cake or a scone maybe?"

I gave her a small smile back and shook my head.

"I'm good thanks."

"No? Ok. Well how about this?" She wrote something down on her notepad and slipped it infront of me.

I looked up at her and she grinned.

"I think you're cute. We should hang out some time."

I chuckled and she frowned a little.

"What?"

"Nothing."

I finished my coffee while she went back to her work.

I watched her; the way she interacted with people, the smile she forced when she had to be nice to some idiotic person and how she would tease and laugh with her collegues. She was happy.

I got up, leaving a tip on the table next to the empty coffee mug and her number and left the coffee shop.

As I walked down the road, I heard the door open and stopped walking, knowing that when I turned around, Natasha would be half frowning, half smirking at me.

"Hey, cute girl!"

I bit back a grin and turned around.

She arched an eyebrow at me.

"That's a bit egotistical of you; how do you know I was calling out for you?"

I shrugged.

"You said I was cute?"

She laughed.

"Ok, fair play. So, why didn't you take my number? Am I not your type?"

I looked her up and down, thinking back on all the time we'd spent together.

"Oh trust me you are, but have you ever had a feeling that you'd already been somewhere before?"

She frowned, clearly not understanding me.

"Not really... and I'm not someone who you can only have once, if you know what I mean." And she winked for good measure.

I grinned without showing my teeth.

"Still, be that as it may, it won't work out, Natasha."

I turned and walked away from her.

"Wait...how do you know my name?"

"Oh I don't know, from another life maybe?"

THE END

WRITTEN BY JAYDEN KANE

Note from the author: First of all, dear reader, thank you so much for choosing this book. I write stories in the hope that people can read them and relate to the characters in some form or another and this can help them to handle whatever it is they are dealing with or maybe you just want a good book to pick up and enjoy.

I hope to write more stories like this and maybe even branch out into the more romantic comedy side of fiction...we'll see.

Anyway, once again, thank you for reading and if you liked this book, feel free to leave a review on Amazon.

All my Love,

Jayden x

Acknowledgement: I'd like to thank my Mum. You always listened to my stories and made me a better writer. This one is for you, because I feel I owe it to you to at least have one book out there, just like you wanted.

I hope I continue to make you proud, Mum. Love you, Always and Forever x

About the Author: Jayden Kane was born and raised in London. She has always loved writing and bringing different characters to life. When she's not writing, Jayden likes to spend time with her friends and her brother.
She loves dark lesbian fantasy novels, thrillers and walks out in nature.

Social Media: Instagram as JaydenKaneWriter08

Printed in Great Britain
by Amazon

41808501R00061